## Books by Kathryn Lively

*ExStream Love*

Finish What You Started
Drive Me Wild

Drive Me Wild

ISBN # 978-1-78686-300-3

©Copyright Kathryn Lively 2017

Cover Art by Posh Gosh ©Copyright 2017

Interior text design by Claire Siemaszkiewicz

Totally Bound Publishing

Published in 2017 by Totally Bound Publishing, Think Tank, Ruston Way, Lincoln, LN6 7FL, United Kingdom.

Totally Bound Publishing is a subsidiary of Totally Entwined Group Limited.

ExStream Love

# DRIVE ME WILD

KATHRYN LIVELY

# Dedication

Dedicated to the memory of Joe Ann Lively.

# Chapter One

Of all the awards to be given away tonight, she had to present *this* one. Why? What unseen universal force sought to punish and taunt her?

Steffi Corden stood just off stage and squirmed in her strapless Herve Leger gown, which felt half a size too tight since the last time she'd tried it on. The compressed bodice of the otherwise flowing dress made everything she wore underneath just as uncomfortable. She twisted in place while somebody — she missed the winner's name and didn't recognize the guy, a writer in the limited series category, she guessed — kept the crowd's attention with his rambling acceptance speech.

*Gads!* She had a wire — more like a needle — protruding from her bra and jabbing her underboob area. Steffi searched backstage, checking for gawkers and wondering if anybody would notice if she dipped her hand down her cleavage and ripped the offending garment away. Just her luck if somebody strolled by with a phone extended, creating a Snapchat story while they caught her fondling herself in public.

Her agent's admonition, however, sounded in her memory. Suzan had been a costume designer in her previous life and as such finished the dress alterations at no cost to her. *Whatever you got on under this thing now, wear it to the show*, she'd warned. *Unless you want a wardrobe malfunction to define your career.*

*Heh.* Given how things were going at the moment, a little tit flash in front of the academy and eleven million at-home viewers wouldn't be the worst thing to happen to her this month. Maybe she'd get a movie offer out of it.

In the distance, music swelled, and the winner's voice pitched high to speak over the shrill strings. After a final fist pump in the air, award clutched at the base, he took the arm of the lovely young awards escort and strolled Steffi's way.

Presenter Tripp Wallace, who'd guested on Steffi's show in the first episode, loped behind the duo and offered her a wink as he passed.

"Good luck," he whispered. "They're all staring at their phones."

*I would, too.* Point her to the nearest bar and wake her when all this ended. *Gah! This frickin' wire stabbing at my breast!* Shimmying didn't relieve the pain.

Lord, but she hated award shows—one necessary evil in her industry. Had she not come tonight to accept the Best Actress in a Drama Series statuette—assuming she'd win—the public might think her a snob, or else figure she didn't want to share breathing space with her ex, Dash Gregory, and his new wife. The higher-ups at ExStream, the online streaming network where TV viewers could binge on her drama, *ViP*, might equate a snub to disrespecting the company. She was already in hot water with them. The first season of *ViP*, starring Steffi as the Vice President of the United States, failed to bring in the numbers they'd hoped for. Of the four original programs to debut in the last year, they had ordered new episodes for all shows but hers.

*Danse Macabre*, a dark fantasy about a motorcycle-riding Grim Reaper, starred her ex-boyfriend and attracted record viewership for ExStream. That morning Steffi had read on her phone how the network had commissioned an unprecedented three additional seasons from Too True Productions, helmed by former child star and current television wunderkind Gabby Randall.

AKA Mrs. Dash Gregory.

Bitch.

Gabby had everything she wanted—the man, the success, and in a few minutes she might get the award, too. Steffi looked down at the envelope in her hand, for Best Writing in a Drama Series.

Gabby's category.

Thanks to a few ill-timed tweets made by Steffi earlier in the year—beefing about Dash rekindling a romance with Gabby, his former *Wondermancer High* co-star from when both were teen idols—it seemed the whole world followed Steffi's personal and professional decline with glee. She guessed the sadistic asshole responsible for planning this event intended to extend her humiliation by placing her on stage with her ex-lover's new wife.

Because Gabby would win this damn award. She deserved it. *Danse Macabre* was sex on a stick, hot and crack-tastic. Every episode was the Super Bowl, the *Lost* finale and the ratings-gold bullet in Tony Soprano's head, all rolled into a hot fudge sundae. All that and Dash's super-fine naked ass as the cherry on top.

*Danse* came into this year's awards with twenty-five nominations to *ViP*'s eight. Most of those were techie honors handed out at an earlier ceremony, but they still counted, and *Danse* had picked up a few more wins tonight. Steffi's Best Actress nomination proved one of the few bright spots in an otherwise dreary year for her, and though she ought to be excited for her first prime-time acting nomination, she felt nauseated.

She put thoughts of winning or losing out of her head. Tried to. The idea that a win for *ViP* saved her show from cancellation gave her some hope for her future.

A woman with a clipboard and an earpiece appeared by her side. "Ms. Corden, sixty seconds." She disappeared before Steffi acknowledged her.

*Right. Shoulders straight. Deep breath. Smile. Look for the teleprompter near the lighted camera. Don't think about the poking sensation under your left boob and the blood that's probably trickling down your torso and staining the inside of this two-thousand-dollar dress you'll never wear again.*

The first few notes of *ViP*'s theme exploded from the

orchestra pit, and Steffi walked out to center stage amid polite applause. She'd presented major awards before, but only at the separate ceremony for daytime programming, back when she'd starred on a popular soap. This didn't seem any different—just more TV viewers being kind to her on social media as they live-tweeted, she hoped.

She focused on the camera. From where she stood, she had trouble making out faces so it seemed pointless to seek out Dash and Gabby to gauge their reaction to her. The clapping died down along with the music and Steffi put on her star face.

"A vigilante confronts her mother's killer. A husband discovers his spouse's deceit. A sexual assault trial takes an unexpected turn. A warrior finds a new ally in the battle for supremacy against another planet. And, a detective takes a crucial step toward arresting a mysterious biker outlaw. These five stories kept television viewers on the edges of their seats this year, and tonight one of their writers will be recognized for their exemplary work."

*Whew.* She'd gotten out the hard words with no fumbles. Steffi paused, her head bowed slightly while the faceless show announcer read the names of all the nominees. *ViP*, despite acting nominations and the Best Drama nod, had been shut out of this category. Nothing for her to root for here. *How in the hell did our show final in all the major cats but this one? Too many channels, too many options now,* she decided.

A second round of applause followed, bringing her back to the awards, and Steffi tugged at the envelope. Whoever had sealed it must have used super glue. One wrong move and she'd slice her wrist.

Steffi gave a short laugh, sensing the crowd's tension. No pressure, just the entire free world watching her bumble like a fool. She released a breath and the flap came loose.

"And the award goes to…" Her voice pitched high, then the air left her when she saw the name on the card.

*Ah, crap. I knew it.*

"Gabby Randall, for *Danse Macabre*."

*'It's a great opportunity,'* she had said. *'You'll make connections in the industry,'* she had said. *'Chances are high they'll put you next to a producer and you can work your charm during commercial breaks,'* she said.

Barry Spahn sat in the fifth row and fumed. Almost everything his friend Mags had told him about the seat-filler gig turned out to be bullshit. Mags worked for a casting company responsible for finding warm bodies for this and similar events. One would think this town was full of starving actors interested in the opportunity, and when Mags had called him at the eleventh hour crying for his help he should have suspected something was up.

There was a reason Hollywood hopefuls didn't flock to warm seats vacated by famous butts. For one, the job paid squat. He also had to furnish the tux and transportation to the venue *and* find a place to park — no limo escorts for the little people — and when he had arrived at the employee entrance a stern countenanced woman with a clipboard had thrust an NDA in his face to sign while she'd rattled off a list of rules.

*'Sit where we tell you, shut up and get up when prompted.'*

*'No talking to any of the celebrities, or other nominees, their dates, their relatives or anybody else who paid to come here. Shut up.'*

*'No texting, no tweeting, no selfies, no kidding.'*

Why would Mags lie about the particulars of this gig? *Don't answer that, brain.* Mags needed help with her job. He was a sucker with a white knight complex. A perfect fit.

So he was out the suit rental and gas, worrying about the security of his car parked several blocks away, and unable to network. He got over the 'shut up' part of tonight without issues, but anxiety about his car ate at his insides. His car was his livelihood at the moment, and if it got towed he was screwed.

Barry had mentally kicked himself for not asking about

pay first thing. After he had accepted the job, though, Mags had played the guilt card for hours and promised to help jumpstart his career any way she could. Fine and good, but if he had to pay a towing company's ransom Mags better have cash on hand.

With the show slouching toward an end, he decided not to hold high hopes on getting a check, given how Mags had neglected to tell him everything else about this 'volunteer' bit. He wanted to cut his losses and go home, but the last rule on the NDA burned in his head from the moment they had gone live. *Any seat filler caught breaking a rule or behaving in a manner unbecoming to the academy will be ejected from the ceremony, and the person responsible for hiring said offender will be dismissed from his/her position.*

*Play nice, or Mags collects unemployment.* Mags with the mortgage and two fatherless children. He did not want that on his conscience.

So, he sat in various spots throughout the evening until the coordinator parked him in the fifth row by the aisle. Twenty minutes and counting until the final goodnight, assuming the show didn't run overtime. He had no idea whose place he'd taken, but he assumed the person had grown bored with the lame jokes and predictable wins and had slipped away to some bar, like he wanted to do right now. He'd given up precious writing time for a false alarm, and had he been plagued with a creativity block, he could have taken on a few rideshare jobs and earned some much-needed green.

Instead, he sat, his discomfort increasing with every second the cougar in the plunging V-neck gown perched next to him attempted to chat him up.

He struggled to recall where he'd seen her before. Sitting this close to the stage, she had to be *somebody*. Perhaps a nominee in a non-acting category, a person whose face wasn't showcased on the big screen during presentations. She was rail thin and leathery tan, rocking a smoky eye and pink streaks in her dirty-blonde crop cut. She observed no boundaries, touching his arm and shoulder when she laughed at every damn thing out of the host's mouth. Hot gravel stirred in a popcorn popper.

*Where do I know you from, lady?* Mags might know. Too bad he couldn't snap a quick shot and text her. Mags watched all those Real Housewife-type shows, from Atlanta to Zanzibar. This woman resembled one to him. Especially when she opened her big mouth.

While he kept fast to the shut up slash eyes straight rule, his seat buddy leaned close and whispered in his ear, "I got two words for you—Jennifer Aniston."

*No, I don't think you're her.* He side-eyed her and tried a smile. The tux, buttoned to the hilt, constricted him and he baked in his chair while a comedic ingénue announced the winner of the Best Writing in a Limited Series award.

A man—maybe a teenager, he wore high-top sneakers with his suit and looked as though a razor never had to touch his baby-skinned face—sprinted up the steps amid applause for his trophy. Barry guessed nepotism had gotten the winner this far. He had the vibe of a nephew with connections, handed a golden ticket.

Barry's neighbor, by contrast, held a mischievous gleam in her dark-rimmed eyes.

"You know who's up next? The person you're subbing for." An arm inked with a string of kanji down the underside crossed his line of vision as the woman pointed toward backstage. "I got a feeling you should make yourself comfortable. She ain't coming back. She don't like me much."

*I wonder why.* Barry nodded, and smiled. Mouth shut. If there was a rule against listening while a celebrity or other person prattled on and on, the coordinator had neglected to advise him of such. He'd missed whoever vacated this seat when he'd taken it—saw only her retreating form as an escort guided her backstage, so he found the clue useless.

He eliminated Jennifer Aniston, who wasn't here tonight. If his instincts were correct, though. Yep, seat buddy opened her mouth again.

"Can you believe the balls of whoever parsed out these presenting gigs?" Hot gravel in his ear now. "If Gabby wins this, she's going to receive the award from her husband's ex-girlfriend."

*Ah.* He might have spent the last year or so sequestered in his apartment writing when he wasn't working, but even he emerged from the cave once in a while to catch up on trends and issues. So Steffi Corden was up after this next commercial break to give out the Best Writing in a Drama Series accolade. A flutter of envy over Gabby Randall's nomination passed through him. He normally didn't track television awards but he paid attention to all things writing in the industry, and though he'd only seen a few episodes of the series Gabby had created, he'd been enthralled by the dialogue and pacing.

He'd crushed on Gabby once upon a time, as a fan of her old vehicle *Wondermancer High*. She'd played one of the popular girl wizards on the show about a magical high school. He understood young actors involved in cult series had trouble breaking the stereotypes, or finding subsequent performance work at all. Gabby, like Ron Howard and Jodie Foster before her, had proved an exception by moving behind the camera and hitting big. Her leading man Dash Gregory, mired in stereotype city as *Wondermancer High's* token geek, had seemed headed for obscurity until she'd cast him in the very different role of Reaper.

He could only hope for a career half as successful as theirs. Hell, if he had the chance to write one episode of *Danse Macabre* he'd leap at it.

Any TV show. Something besides carting around actors on the way to auditions and slash or the unemployment office while they spilled drinks and broke wind in his car.

"She's the new Jennifer Aniston," the woman next to him said. "Gabby's Angelina."

"Ah." *Well, hell.* Heart in his throat, he searched the immediate area for the clipboard lady. Then he pressed his fist to his mouth and coughed to cover up his error.

He recalled seeing Dash Gregory trending in social media during his turbulent romance with the actress. Fans would catch them brawling in restaurants and create looped videos of nails scratching, glass flying, four-letter terms of non-endearment screeched. Mostly on Steffi's part, for Dash was too busy ducking and dodging.

His neighbor quieted down as Steffi announced the category, and he applauded for each nominee, then winced when his seat buddy whooped at mention of Gabby. When the actress called out Gabby's name as the winner a collective cry of elation filled the auditorium but he kept his eye on Steffi, ashen and thoroughly defeated. The girl at the school dance passed over by the quarterback for the head cheerleader.

Well, maybe that wasn't a good analogy. You were supposed to root for the wallflower, who would bloom in the third act and win everybody's approval. Everybody in Hollywood knew Steffi had brought most of her ill fortune on herself with her bad behavior.

Gabby shook Steffi's hand, accepted her award and turned her attention to the crowd. "Wow, thank you so much," she gushed, radiant with an expression of shock. "This is a surprise. As long as I've been in television, I've dreamed of standing here. Never thought it would be for writing, but I'll gladly take it."

A ripple of laughter erupted. Barry's seat buddy squawked and clasped her hands together, more into this moment than anyone else. He figured the lady had spent a fair amount of time before the show at the VIP green room, partaking of the free booze. She was tripping.

"I want to thank ExStream for having faith in the show," Gabby continued, "to Lina DeVito and everybody at Too True Productions for their hard work and support and Randi Marsh for her exceptional directing in this now award-winning episode."

Somebody in the upper level let out a rebel yell and

Gabby's speech faltered. The lady next to him twisted in place to search for the offender. "You hear that?" She smacked Barry's arm so hard he expected a bruise. "I got a fan."

At those words, his memory jarred. He stopped himself from snapping his fingers, certain it was also against the rules — he hadn't read the NDA word for word before signing it.

*Holy cow.* He hadn't recognized Randi Marsh, AKA Randi Raucous — eighties glam metal queen and occasional actress. In her prime, Randi had ranked among the top female rock musicians — Joan, Lita, Wendy O., Randi. Barry recalled the poster his brother had pinned to his bedroom wall, highlighting curvy Miss Marsh clad only in strategically placed strips of electric tape, spread-eagle over a giant Gibson Flying V guitar as if she was about to ride it to the moon. After the rock glory had faded, Randi had appeared on Gabby's old show from time to time, playing a relative or something.

Eccentric bisexual rebel, so the tabloid sites claimed, but she had connections. Gabby Randall freakin' name-checked her in her speech… She directed television shows, and the clipboard lady forbade him to talk back. *Damn it!*

He half-listened to Gabby's acceptance speech. "Thank you, Emma and Charlie, Tania and Janie, the rest of the cast and crew. Too many names to get into here, but expect a long blog post later," she said. "Lastly, there's one special person I must thank. I am here, and *Danse Macabre* is here tonight, because of Dashiell Gregory, my star and my husband."

A smattering of applause followed and Barry noticed Steffi's eye roll. The camera projecting on the big screen focused only on the winner, but Barry smirked at the thought of somebody catching Steffi's reaction. It was the stuff of GIF loops shared for years on Twitter.

"Dash, you are a truly remarkable actor and I am thrilled the world sees what I've known all along. I love you. Thank you all." Gabby hoisted the award over her head in salute to her show, her crew and her husband, then started for backstage with Steffi several steps behind, her shoulders hunched.

For a fleeting moment, he felt sorry for the other actress. Like Randi had said, the moment represented a passing of a torch Steffi didn't want to surrender. Not long ago she'd enjoyed a successful run on a daytime soap, then a network show and a cute boyfriend...albeit one drowning in on-demand and direct-to-video schlock. Perhaps his career downswing had attracted her, gave her an advantage in the relationship.

Now she loped behind a true victor, but the night wasn't over. They still had the Best Actress in a Drama and Best Drama categories coming, and Steffi's show had a shot at both of those awards.

Another commercial break. Seat fillers popped up and skittered out of sight. The clipboard lady barged down the center aisle, corralling loose people and directing them to newly vacated seats. Barry glanced at his watch—nearly eight o'clock, close to after-party time. Not that he'd been invited to any. On the East Coast, millions of viewers like his family in Florida were probably sacked out on their couches waiting for the agony to end.

"You ain't much of a talker, are you, seat warmer?" Randi asked. He turned to her and caught the gleam in her steely eyes. She was testing him, he realized. He figured she'd been to enough of these shows to know the seat filler rules and, seeing as how she didn't win her category tonight, figured messing with the help made up for it.

"Fuck, I'm just yanking your chain." Randi laughed. "I gotta admit, though, I'm having a better time with you than I would have had I brought a date. I do like the silent type.

"Last guy I took to one of these things, we were right behind Kate Hudson and he kept flipping her hair. She thought *I* was doing it, and giving me all these dirty looks." She leaned in with a conspiratorial wink. "Course, that might've been because she thinks I flinged with her dad once, or one of her uncles. I can't keep 'em straight."

He wanted to speak, actual words. He'd been quiet all night, and feared if he opened his mouth he'd squeak from drought. He contemplated a possible penalty for himself or Mags if he slipped a business card from his wallet and handed it to the woman with a wide-eyed expression that read *Please pass this along to your best friend, Gabby Randall.* He licked his lips but the clipboard lady passed close and his body went rigid.

Randi slouched in her seat, straightening the spaghetti straps of her bodice. "Smart boy," she murmured.

Camera on, cue to applause. Last year's Best Actor in a Drama Series winner walked onstage to present the counterpart award. As with the previous acting award, each nominee received a fifteen-second spotlight on the big screen, a scene from the episode which netted them the honor then another quick round of applause. They were presented alphabetically, and the camera panned to Steffi standing backstage after her clip, eyes wide like a frightened rabbit's, before moving on to the rest of the ladies.

"And the award goes to…" This time the presenter ripped through the envelope like onion skin. No fuss, no muss. "Dedra Worth, for *District Two.*"

The brassy theme to the popular cop drama started up and the screen filled with Dedra's surprised reaction to her win. Elegant in a slim-fitting purple gown with spangled straps, she rose from her front row seat to claim her trophy. Barry watched from where he realized he'd sit for the rest of the program. He couldn't see if Steffi still lingered where she'd stood, but he imagined the defeat had hit her like a punch to the gut. He wouldn't blame her for seeking out the green room and drowning her sorrows in a drink.

Lord knew he was ready for a belt or five himself.

# Chapter Two

*Shit, motherfucker, penis, tits. Fuckin' strike me dead right now.*

Steffi remained still for about a minute, clapping with strained politeness while Dedra Worth took her sweet time blubbering and hugging everybody within touching distance. It wouldn't look right if somebody had kept a camera trained on her as she stormed off in disgust. In a way, though, she was happy for her fellow actress's win. Academy voters proved predictable once again in choosing a performance dealing with a controversial topic, but it didn't mean Dedra was undeserving of the win.

On *District Two*, Dedra played a homicide detective on trial for shooting a man who had sexually assaulted her daughter. Steffi won her award nomination for an episode where her Vice President character debated whether or not to tell her advisors she might have cancer. By the program's end, it turned out to be a false alarm and everybody went back to work. Not the most intense material written for her, but she cried a lot and kicked a trash can through a window in one scene, and she figured the realistic tantrum put her in the final five.

In truth, she'd thought of Dash and Gabby while filming that near field goal. *Use your pain and, oh, the places you'll go.*

Well, there was always next year...all she needed was a show. The fate of *ViP* seemed less secure with another award loss, leaving their last hope hinging on the top prize. Steffi decided she wanted to stand somewhere else while that envelope was opened.

She shuffled on aching feet to the green room, a backstage

setup for presenters and other special ticket holders to relax and enjoy a snack or a glass of something strong. A few sympathetic smiles followed her, and she held her head high. People expected a meltdown, and why not? When Dash had signed on for the role of Reaper on *Danse Macabre* last year, she'd suggested on Twitter that his past romantic connection to producer Gabby had influenced the decision more than his acting skills. Big mistake. The TV-loving public, most of them *Wondermancer High* fans who probably still owned the dolls and battery-operated wands, had spanked her good on that.

Then *Danse Macabre* had smoked every other show in the ExStream original programming schedule and netted several trophies during the night, including one for Dash. Despite that, she'd been partly right about the two. They were in love, probably had been since they'd met up again, even after their first shot at a relationship had failed.

How many lovers of 'Dabby' came back and said to Steffi, "Well, you might have been right all along?" Zip. People sided with winners.

Inside a wood-paneled lounge flush with comfortable seating and tables heavy with *hors d'oeuvres,* Steffi strode to the bar and ordered a Jack and Ginger. She slipped a tenner into the tip glass and shotgunned the cocktail before the spherical ice could bead up.

*Slam.* She set the glass back onto the bar with force and followed it with a glare at the wide-eyed boy in the rent-a-tux manning the booze. Steffi signaled for a refill and startled when a hand touched on her shoulder. Tania Pope wore an emerald-green bandage dress with low heels, her hair done up in Princess Leia buns. "Stef, have you tried these chicken skewers? Delish. They're breaded with corn flakes, and the chili mustard is addictive."

She ought to eat something, she knew. Fear of not being able to fit into her dress kept her away from food most of the day, and she should have something to balance the alcohol. The thought of chicken and chili mustard nauseated her, more so when she thought of Dedra Worth chatting with the press while hugging her award.

She sipped long on her second drink, watching the young actress in front of her chow down on a clear plastic plate full of nibbles. Tania was what one called a perennial guest star, the girl everybody recognized as 'that chick or 'that gal', but whose name escaped memory. She'd appeared on Steffi's old soap a few times and, several months ago, worked on *Danse Macabre*. How she managed the clout to breach this exclusive space, Steffi couldn't say. Steffi would bet Tania had come with an A-lister date.

Steffi preferred to drink and wallow alone. *Eh, what the hell. Might as well act charitable tonight.* "I get a nervous stomach at these things. Can't eat. Ginger ale helps." She raised her glass.

"Right. Ginger ale." Tania winked and downed a mushroom puff.

"What are you up to?"

Tania chewed and nodded, then swallowed. "Leaving for New York tomorrow for six weeks. Off-Broadway show. You going back to *ViP*?"

"I'll be there." *Not sure about the rest of the cast and crew. Or if the doors will be padlocked.*

"Ooh, we're back on." Tania pointed her plate toward the large flat-screen on the far wall, where a number of guests had gathered. "I was on the ep of *Dysfunctional* nominated tonight."

"Cool." Steffi didn't give a damn about the Best Comedy Series award. Like a win would cause Tania's career to skyrocket, but it gave the girl an emotional boost when the show won. Tania whooped and sent bite-sized crackers airborne.

Steffi leaned back toward the bartender and held up one finger, then pointed down at her now empty glass. She ignored his silent head shake. *Don't judge. At least you have a job.*

"Good luck," Tania chirped, and sidled away to the side

of an actor Steffi recognized as a pussy hound.

"You, too," she said in a quiet voice, knowing Tania would benefit more from penicillin than luck with that dude. Onscreen, the legendary Lucille Krofft—a woman whose career started when television was invented and watched in dozens of homes nationwide—crept toward the podium on the arm of dark-suited eye candy. Steffi finished her drink while the actress croaked her introduction to the Best Drama award.

"And the nominees are…" Logos for *Covington Place, Danse Macabre, District Two, Game On* and *ViP* flashed in rapid succession before the camera focused back on Lucille. The old woman yanked at the gilded envelope, and if one looked closely they'd see she had the wrong end.

"Jeez, lady," Steffi murmured, "break the seal on the back. It's right there."

Lucille's escort, watching her struggle, had to step forward and assist. The actress squinted at the card with a frown indicating her lack of recognition. "*Danse Macabre*," she trilled, pronouncing it *mack-ob-bray.*

The VIP room erupted with joy. Butts lifted out of seats in the auditorium for a standing ovation. Cast and crew of the winning show clustered in the aisle for a group hug.

Steffi, fuming, ordered one more for the road.

* * * *

"What are you doing? Hey!"

*Ah, heck.* He'd opened his mouth again. Spoke to Randi Marsh. Like he had a choice. The woman had damn near kicked him into the aisle trying to get out of the row. He understood she had to join the rest of the crew onstage to accept the big award, but she couldn't wait two lousy seconds for him to rise and give her a wider berth?

Had the clipboard lady seen it? He thought at first it wouldn't matter much, seeing as how the show would shut down after the final speech and the host's goodnight.

Still, even a last-minute breaking of a rule might lead to a penalty, and Mags resorting to buying generic brands of groceries to save money. Opening her home to boarders to pay the bills. Selling hair and blood.

*Eh, it's L.A.* She'd find work somewhere else.

After a moment, he managed to straighten up and he stood by his aisle seat, waiting for Randi to slide past. When she looped her arm in his and pulled him forward, he yelped a protest.

"What're you doing?" He pushed out the words through too-close lips, his teeth clenched. If the clipboard lady had a camera trained on him, he wanted as many facial muscles as possible frozen to prove he'd kept up his end of the deal.

"My show won, man. I can't be seen up there without a *date*." Randi tugged harder, dislodging his stance. Before he realized it, he was another tuxedo thrust into the throng of celebrating actors, writers and other crew. Hands slapped his back, lips touched down on his cheeks and an ecstatic Dash Gregory hugged him.

*Surreal.* He'd become flotsam in a wave of people moving toward the stage, and he felt neither the carpet nor the hard floor as he joined the *Danse Macabre* party onstage, gathered around Gabby Randall as she began speaking.

*Crap.* What if somebody noticed him up here and realized he had nothing to do with the show? Randi's arm stayed locked with his, but her attention called to the upper balcony and fans calling out her name. Barry bowed his head in an attempt to obscure his face and eased behind a black woman dressed in light blue.

*It's fine.* He'd stopped talking. Nothing in the rules list about not getting up onstage with winners, not that he'd read. He'd point out that loophole in the event the seat filler committee, or whoever organized this stuff, tried to pin this on Mags and get her fired.

"Seriously, this has been one amazing ride," Gabby was saying. "I couldn't ask for better writers, directors, editors, cameramen…the hair and makeup and special effects. I know I'm going to leave somebody out. There's Dash and Emma and Randi." Gabby looked back for a second and her eyes connected with his. She blinked a moment and his heart stopped. He prayed in his head for her to pass over him and continue her congratulatory roll call.

She recovered after a second and went on, allowing him to breathe easy again. For about two seconds.

"Hang on now."

The other voice talked over Gabby's and sounded distant. Randi muttered an "Oh, hell," in his ear and Barry turned to see Steffi Corden charging up the stage toward the group. Behind her, one of the stage escorts stepped forward as if to stop her, yet paused with his arm outstretched for a moment before backing up.

Wild-eyed and flushed, Steffi wobbled a few steps—unsure on her heels until she winced and kicked them free. One skittered to the lip of the stage.

"Dear God, she's pulling a Kanye," somebody on his other side said.

"Hey, don't hate on Kanye," Randi barked.

Gabby quieted, and Dash pressed close as though to buffer his wife. Steffi charged up to them anyway and put her face right in the mic. "You'll get your show back in a minute. I just have to say something," Steffi spoke in a voice too loud for the moment. Bystanders winced. Barry couldn't see well into the audience for the lights, but detected some discomforted shifting in the front row. The melody of faint strings from the orchestra pit—a warning noise to cut an overlong speech—rose into the air in an apparent attempt to discourage Steffi from showing her ass.

No such luck. "I think this is the first time a streaming network has won Best Drama, so yay for ExStream," Steffi continued. "I think it's cool a woman-run show is a winner tonight, too." Applause erupted and when she spoke again. "You should know, though, ExStream isn't a one-show pony."

Dash leaned over to speak in Steffi's ear. The mic failed to catch his words, but Steffi glared at him and made to slap away any placating gestures. "Watch it, bub. I got pictures on the cloud you don't want anybody to download."

Dash shrank back. Gabby's expression withered. Barry side-eyed his 'date' and winced at Randi's glee. The woman loved a good train wreck, that was clear, and Steffi had long ago run off the rails. This had to stop before another embarrassing thing happened. The woman was drunk, unstable and baring her misery to the free world. Why had no security come to lead her away? That escort could have nabbed her and pulled her back into the wings, right?

He eased away from Randi and apologized. "Excuse me," he whispered, and edged in between gowns and suits to get right behind Gabby, who stood with the Best Drama trophy looking lost and worried. Steffi continued to babble about giving other shows on ExStream a chance, and his heart ached for her in that moment. He tried to keep up with the industry and had heard rumblings about show cancelations. He'd never been involved in a series himself, but he understood rejection and failure enough to sympathize with the woman.

This stunt, however, guaranteed a producer considering Steffi for a project might move on to the next actress in line.

"Excuse me," he muttered to Gabby, and the woman stepped to one side. He'd committed a grave seat filler sin by standing here, he assumed, so why not go big before going home? At best, he hoped for somebody to get his name wrong in the media so it wouldn't affect the screenwriting career he wanted to launch.

"I believe in *ViP*, and ExStream. It is a new way for original programming," Steffi babbled with her focus on the ever-rumbling audience. "That's not to say the networks are dead. I got my start on network and I love you guys, too. All those great shows like…"

She stopped. Had she suffered a brain fart on live television? If so, silent and deadly. Oh, not a good time to *stop* talking, especially if you can't think of one show airing on the Big Three this year.

"Anyway, please give *ViP* a chance. A lot of shows don't hit their stride until the second season, anyway, and I need one for that to happen." Steffi's voice cracked.

*Okay, Steffi, time to go.* Barry came to her side, debating whether or not he ought to guide her away from the mic. In her state, there was no telling how she'd react. He cleared his throat before she took a breath to speak again. "Miss Corden, thank you. I believe Mrs. Gregory would like to say a few more words."

*Damn.* He'd said that into the mic. Everybody had heard him. His voice had sounded strange to his own ears. Should he have referred to her as Ms. Randall?

This no doubt counted as talking to people. Somewhere in the dark recesses of the auditorium, the clipboard lady probably lost her shit.

Steffi jerked her head and glared at him. "Who are you?"

Were his relatives and friends back in Florida watching this? He envisioned the web of texts between his sisters and mother, her sisters and his cousins. What about social media? Maybe he trended now. #WhosTheWeirdo

"Uh, I've been asked to assist you—"

"By who, Mrs. *Gregory*?" Steffi scoffed and turned her venom on to Dash, whose face expressed his slow burn. "I was right all along about your work ethic. I bet Gabby didn't bother with any other auditions once she—"

Barry anticipated her next words would sting. Somebody needed to silence her for her own good. With no time to think, he did the one thing guaranteed to shut her down without making it look like an assault.

He pulled Steffi close and planted a kiss on her parted lips. No tongue, no passion, just a hard press to prevent an insult she'd no doubt regret later. He kept his eyes open the whole, brief time and noticed hers widened to saucers. She struggled for a second before moaning a protest, and when it appeared he'd subdued her, she yanked back and shoved him away.

In the background, Randi brayed.

"What is wrong with you, buddy?" Steffi wiped her mouth with the back of her arm. Good question. In two seconds, he could become the most popular man on earth. Not in a good way, either.

"You need help getting her out of here?" Dash asked him. "I think you're doing it wrong."

Barry saw the actor's hands flex into fists. The whole world watched, waited. A few people heckled and clapped. Somebody had to move before this hot mess escalated into a brawl. When Dash edged closer he knocked Barry forward, causing him to grasp Steffi for balance. He caught her by the shoulders, but she shrugged away with a grunt.

"No more freebies. I'm going. Jeez. Enjoy it while it lasts, Randall." With a final snarl at the nearest bystanders, Steffi stormed off and Barry pursued her past the stage curtain and into the spacious backstage area. Behind him Gabby's voice echoed—she made no mention of the interruption and soldiered on with her acceptance speech, picking up from where Steffi had horned in on the celebration. Class act, but he had no time to contemplate it.

Without her heels, Steffi managed to cover a lot of ground, and with various crew milling about Barry lost track of her.

"Where's Steffi Corden?" he called out. Nothing prepared him for backstage at an awards show. Every path led to somewhere specific, he soon discovered. Winners had to take one route to a backstage media room where cameras rolled and flashed and reporters shouted over each other to be heard. Somebody spotted him and shouted out for his name and his relationship to Steffi. There must have been a closed-circuit monitor in there airing the show, otherwise why bother with him? He backed away to search elsewhere.

Another avenue took presenters and nominees to a green room for drinking and sulking. Still another to bathrooms and a designated smoking area, where Barry sniffed out something medicinal and legal only in a few states.

He took a good whiff before somebody noticed and

guided him toward a back exit. Since he'd not found Steffi anywhere else, he deduced she'd Hulk-smashed her way outside. Did she hold some poor usher hostage? The soles of his only pair of dress shoes echoed in the concrete hallway as he ran. It sounded like a lonely business, his search for the disgraced starlet.

All the while, he wondered, why only him? He had no stake in ensuring Steffi's safety, but he remembered his parents' admonishments to act helpful toward others. Funny how nobody else in the vicinity seemed to give a damn.

The exit led him out to a side entrance of the theater building—an area crowded with onlookers and no clear path to the front. He'd been given a pass before arriving for the ceremony, and he kept it in hand as he shouldered through security and backstage crew and assorted hangers-on until he reached a velvet rope cordoning off the red carpeted entrance from the great unwashed. The card was color-coded, and he had no idea if green granted him permission to prowl this part of building, but nobody bothered him.

A few celebrity reporters from various entertainment shows paced the sheltered entrance to the theater, presumably on simultaneous commercial breaks as they checked makeup and hair. Barry spotted one woman he recognized—the pink-haired daughter of a heavy metal legend. She co-hosted a gossip show on E!

"Skylar!" he called out, waving. Skylar's half-shorn head whipped in his direction, and he smiled to give the impression that they knew each other and were on speaking terms. He'd read somewhere on TMZ, or maybe Perez Hilton, that she'd finished a rehab stay. Perhaps whatever she used that put her in a clinic messed with her memory, leaving her to believe she'd been friendly with him at one time.

"Skylar, over here. It's Barry, from…you know." The last words muttered into silence, but the confidence paid off.

Skylar, resplendent in blue genie pants and a matching crop top lined with fringe, beamed and strolled over him. She held a wireless microphone with her network's logo emblazoned underneath the foam covering the speaker.

"Hey, sweetie. Where you been?" She reached over the velvet rope to give him a hug. Holy cow, this was too easy. Best to take advantage before she realized they'd never met before.

"Awesome, love, but we're in a jam. We're almost done in here, and they need Steffi Corden in the media pen for a quick interview. You seen her around? She said something about getting some air."

"Sure haven't, sorry." Skylar's lip pushed out in a pout. "But I haven't looked. They want me to corral Dash and Gabby for an after-show interview, so we're all waiting on them to come out. Did they win?"

"You mean the show? Yeah. Gabby was just giving the speech." Good. If Skylar hadn't seen his on-screen kiss, maybe nobody else outside did, either.

She brightened. "Great, they'll be in a good mood. You'll be at the *Vanity Fair* party later, right?"

*In my dreams.* "Wouldn't miss it."

"Totes cool. We'll catch up." She pressed two fingers against her right ear and grimaced. "I'm back on in twenty. Later, sweetie." Skylar kissed his cheek and strode away. Barry took a deep breath, shocked at how he'd bluffed through that conversation. Perhaps he should consider acting as a backup.

He spied the main entrance and a few attendees came forward to walk the red carpet toward the waiting line of cars at the curb. Cheers erupted from the sidelines, crowded with people who'd stayed to the bitter end to glimpse their favorite stars. Unbelievable. How had these people entertained themselves for the past four hours? One could only take so many selfies in one spot.

He had to come to the auditorium way too early, so he'd missed the big pre-show with all the stars posing and preening. Now, he thought just of going home and forgetting he ever spoke to Mags.

Impossible to ignore now, though, was Steffi Corden wriggling out of a cluster of people coming out of the venue. Somebody must have tried to stall her in the lobby and failed. She argued with a man in a tuxedo, his bowtie and hair askew and her feet bare.

"I am perfectly fine," she shouted, and stumbled back a few steps. None of the reporters stepped in to intervene, and what cameramen roamed the area trained their lenses in her direction as she slapped away arms and shouted curses. Phones lifted high in the air, thumbs tapping at screens to capture the drama.

Fucking vultures. Thank goodness Steffi proved enough of a distraction to let him step over the rope and move to her side.

"Ms. Corden, your car is here," he announced and offered her his arm. He tried to block the cameras' view, pivoting when they turned, and it worked for a few seconds. His appearance seemed to bring some calm to the situation, even to Steffi, who paused in the middle of a stream of four-letter words to regard him.

"Who are you?"

*Really? We spoke five minutes ago. I broke two seat filler commandments. We kissed on live television, for crying out loud.* He straightened his posture and tried to give off an authoritative vibe. A quick glance toward the curb showed him a few limousines ready for pickup. Surely they all led to the same party. If he could get her into one heading in that direction maybe a well-meaning friend would spot her and take over. Those parties were private, so she'd have the space to rant and drink herself silly without judgment.

"I'm here to escort you to your car, Ms. Corden."

She'd ignored his gesture, so he slipped his hand under her arm and took a step closer onto the carpeted path. "If you will come with me—"

"I don't want to go." Steffi sounded like a little girl, whiny and petulant. "I can't show my face anywhere else. They'll all laugh at me."

"Ms. Corden, nobody is laughing at you. Your fans are here for support." Big mistake in gesturing to the crowd. Voices taunted Steffi about Gabby, and some catcalled for her to show off her assets. Unfortunately, he couldn't block sound with his body and Steffi leaned past him to shout back.

"I don't need Dash Gregory! I don't need anybody! I can get my own damn car."

She shoved past him and stomped up the carpet. The media folks surrounding Barry recorded her exit, and somebody within his earshot snickered.

"She'll never do lunch in this town again," one quipped.

"Shit, I think she's about to *lose* her lunch," came a response.

Barry sweltered in his rented suit. It was just after eight, but still light out and the temperature in the high seventies, if the forecast hadn't changed from the afternoon. He wanted nothing more than to get out of touristy Hollywood and into his shower to scrub off this awful experience. Yet, he thought of his friend Mags and the smile of relief on her face when he'd agreed to this gig. He'd saved her bacon, so she said, and despite all the crap he'd endured this evening he knew he'd look back one day and feel good for helping a friend in need.

He'd never encounter Steffi Corden again, he figured, and she didn't know him from any of the bystanders heckling her now. Still, what Catholic guilt remaining in his head and heart nagged at him to take action before the actress did something unforgiveable like, as somebody near him implied, vomit in full view of the public.

He started up the carpet, but Steffi had a solid lead on him. Ahead, a man in full livery stood by an open back passenger door of a purring limo, glancing at Steffi as if unsure of whether or not to let her slide in. For all Barry assumed, the car was reserved for the head of a network or the acting guild, but Steffi surprised them both by wrenching the front passenger door open and diving in headfirst.

"Miss!" called the driver. "You're not supposed to—"

The miss shouted a garbled curse and Barry caught a flash of middle finger. Seconds later, the car lurched forward a few inches and, with both right-side doors still ajar, pulled away from the curb.

"Oh, holy crap," Barry muttered. Steffi Corden had just hijacked a limo at one of the biggest acting award ceremonies in the industry. People gathered around the car leaped for safety as tires screeched and rolled, and when the limo nudged onto the street onlookers screamed and tried to close the swinging car doors.

"My God. Shane, are you getting this?" Skylar cried from behind him. A tall man hefting a TV camera on his shoulder, the assumed Shane, darted forward to capture the getaway. Barry stepped into his path, waving his arms and reaching out to cover the lens.

Shane had a mustache that concealed his upper lip, but there was no mistaking the bared teeth and sneer. "Outta my way, jackass."

"Hey, lay off her, okay? She just lost a major award and her show's in trouble."

"More than her show's in trouble."

"She's had enough, she doesn't need this aired on the news." The anger simmering in Barry's gut spread up his back and into his arms, tightening his hands into fists. He wouldn't dare punch a man with live cameras around, but this person's lack of compassion enraged him. When he'd come to Los Angeles, he'd known to expect impersonal attitudes, but Steffi was a human being. *Damn it.* A public figure, sure, but even the most celebrated of people here deserved a moment of privacy.

Steffi, though, gave the impression she had decided not to cash in that chip. Barry heard a crash and a scream and whirled around to find the limo's front end bent into a signpost. The shiny black hood crinkled into an inverse vee and smoke billowed from the engine. He ran toward the accident scene but the crowd surged forward and pushed him back.

"Is she okay?" he called out. "Is she all right?"

Nobody answered. The street in front of the theater had become all voices and camera phones and speculation.

# Chapter Three

Steffi never wore a watch. As far back as elementary school, when she had learned to tell time, she'd abhorred having anything strapped tight to her wrist. Not even the prospect of owning a My Little Pony model, with her favorite Pinkie Pie's tail as the second hand, tempted her. Despite the lack of a timepiece, Steffi managed to arrive at school, work, wherever, when appointed so. No biggie.

When the fog in her brain lifted and she realized she sat in a gray-barred holding cell, on a thin mattress that reeked of perfume and dried menstrual blood, she wished for a watch to determine how long she'd been left to rot. Last thing she remembered was downing a drink at *Danse Macabre's* final victory at the awards show. Everything after that played like a blurred videotape in her hand. *I pushed somebody, didn't I*, she thought, and shouted down some snide remarks. After that, who knew?

"Fuck me," she muttered, staring down at her feet. She had on nylon slippers, the kind they give you at the shoe store when trying on heels. She wiggled her toes—felt like all ten were intact. Her dress looked okay, but she decided it needed a good cleaning if she stayed on that mattress for much longer.

If Herve Leger saw his design in this condition, and behind bars, he'd probably ban her from wearing anything bearing his label.

She rubbed her neck, which felt sore. *How'd that happen? Why was she here, anyway, and not in a hospital? If she'd been in an accident, then she belonged in one. She reached for her purse and patted an empty, moist spot next to her.

*Ew.*

Her breathing came in short bursts and she surveyed her surroundings. Bars before her and, beyond that, white walls. Silence. No, she heard music in the distance. Sixties surf guitar and falsetto vocals. Not a soul to ask about her past so many hours.

Except that woman in the red leather halter and miniskirt on the other end of the cell, glowering at her.

*Oh, Lord.* Steffi turned her attention away, hoping to discourage a conversation or confrontation. Too little, too late, though. A bone-rattling cough sounded from across the wide cell and Steffi grimaced.

"Your programming is breaking down, itn' it?"

Steffi said nothing. Even a slurred "Huh?" would progress this talk, and she needed her energy to wish for her agent or a lawyer to materialize and get her the hell back to her house. Or to a doctor. She searched her dress for telltale tears to clue her into any unauthorized exploration of everything it covered.

Something scraped the concrete floor, causing her to turn. *Damn it.* She'd made eye contact. Her cellmate—Steffi guessed she was a hooker based on her fishnets and icepick heels and confident strut—popped her chewing gum and smirked as she neared. "I came to L.A. to be an actress, ya know."

Steffi nodded. She'd heard many variations of this story from waitresses and shop clerks, the girl clearing tables at In-N-Out Burger and all the people in between. Nobody came to Hollywood to achieve the dream of a minimum wage job or to walk the streets to make rent. If you didn't have the right combination of talent, drive and pure dumb luck, you settled in until the stars aligned. If at all.

The woman took a seat on the opposite end of the soiled bunk and crossed her legs. Steffi spotted a tattoo of a cross with flowers planted at the base. Dueling aromas from makeup and gum assailed Steffi's nostrils.

"I got a walk-on role in a sitcom after the first month of

auditions," the maybe prostitute continued. "Met a talent agent who thought I'd go far in the business. She said I'd make a great Katniss Everdeen, you know what I mean?"

"Yes." Steffi chose not to mention how her agent had insisted the same of her, how likely every agent in the city fought for their clients for such a plum role. She eyeballed her cellmate at somewhere close to thirty, twice the age of the girl archer character. Of course, she had no idea of this woman's appearance six years ago when the film had been cast…but she imagined the part of Katniss had been locked for Jennifer Lawrence the second the ink had dried on the rights contract. What unknown had a chance?

Her cellmate held up her hand, elbow bracing her thigh, fingers sawing together like she wanted a smoke. "I had a meeting with her after taping that show, and I was escorted into this room with just a table and four chairs. This skeevy-looking bald guy hands me a contract and says everything they'd do for me—all the money and fame, cars, a big house. All I had to do was sign, and that's when I noticed this dagger thingy on the table."

*Oh, nice.* She was one of *those* people. Steffi wondered if this deal with the devil had happened in the woman's head, or in a movie she'd watched while high or drunk.

"They wanted me to sign a fuckin' contract in blood," the women shouted, borderline hysterical now. "And, to show my loyalty to the system, I had to agree to a sacrifice, like have my brother killed in exchange for being a movie star. Who the hell does that?"

Steffi shrugged. Not one of her contracts had called for homicidal extremes. Sure, over the years fans had accused her of being a puppet for the 'elite' cabal of lore believed to rule over Hollywood and the government, and maybe some of the top-tier A-listers in town agreed to casting couch shenanigans to get ahead. Not her. Every success she'd had, she'd worked for it.

She bowed into her hands, rubbing away a headache. To think in the space of a few minutes, she had caused everything in her life to unravel...just because she couldn't accept a few trophy losses with dignity.

"So...who was it?"

Steffi looked up. Her cellmate practically sat in her lap, she was so close.

"What?" she blurted out.

The other woman's head jerked up. "Who'd you have killed to further your career? Was it somebody in your family? Your parents get in a DUI wreck like what's-her-name's did?"

"My parents are alive and well...and why am I talking to you?" Steffi bolted from the bunk and grasped hold of the bars keeping her confined. Still nobody wandered the hall before them, but surely somebody left open an office door to listen for pained screams. "Hey, don't I get a phone call? Can I get some help here?"

"You better repent your sins, Steffi Corden," the prostitute warned. "That all-seeing eye knows what you're up to. Get out while you can."

"And do what? Take up hooking?" Steffi watched the woman bristle at that.

"You've no right to judge me. I may be a whore but I keep up on current events." Dark eyes regarded her with cruel glee. "I know your fella ditched you and your show's circling the drain. If you're thinking of a career change, stay off my corner."

"I'm not interested in slut-shaming you. I got my own problems." *Really? The whole precinct took a coffee break?*

"Damn straight. There's no shame in being a sex worker." The woman folded her arms and huffed. "Especially one as good as me."

"That why you got caught?" Steffi asked.

"The blue laws here are archaic. People get away with all sorts of crap. What's wrong with paying for it? It's your body."

Not that Steffi ever had to pay for that kind of pleasure, but she saw the point. A person could buy cigarettes and alcohol and sugar, all of which brought potential harm if abused, yet scoring a sexual transaction with money landed one in jail. Why not decriminalize sex work? Watch tourism spike.

Steffi shook her head. Strangely enough, talking with this woman helped her anxiety. It got her mind off whatever legal tangle she faced. She might have an episode for *ViP* come out of this if ExStream deigned to save it.

"Well, take care of your body," she told the woman. "You only get one."

"Unless you got a good surgeon."

Steffi snickered at the joke. "I haven't had that done, either, for the record."

She heard footsteps approach. A man in uniform with a bored expression approached with a ring of keys and a raised brow that told Steffi he didn't give a damn about her celebrity. Don't bother with the sweet talk or bribes. "Ms. Corden, your lawyer and your agent have come to collect you," he said and opened the door.

"Thanks." No point in saying more. She'd never been arrested before and knew squat about procedures. Yeah, she'd worked on crime dramas, but refused to accept those scenarios as accurate. Would Suzan escort her to some kind of night court or want reimbursement for bail? Would she have to stand trial for her indiscretions? The cop gave her the impression he wasn't there to fill her in on details.

"Where's *my* agent?" called a voice, still nasal and snotty.

"Shut up, Marleen," barked the cop. "You'll wait on the public defender like you always do."

"C'mon. I'm sure she had a rough night." It came out louder than Steffi intended, and the officer leading her out of the pen stopped short to glare at her. He looked angry enough to throw her back, and she skidded away a few steps. Easy to do in slippered feet.

"We all don't make a million bucks a week, Miss Hollywood." He resumed his heavy lope toward a thick door, Steffi compliant and shaking her head all the way.

*Neither do I, asshole.* What paychecks she'd stashed, though, would afford her a decent lawyer, and she trusted Suzan brought a competent one with her.

Within minutes she shook the hand of one Donald L. Quinton of Quinton and Tyne, Attorneys at Law. Young, dark-skinned, eager and standing about a foot above Steffi's five-five, he spoke in a soothing tone and assured her that she could go home with Suzan tonight. "I'll have all of this handled for you quickly, and I'll come by your home to discuss the particulars. You've had an emotional evening, and I don't see a reason to further exasperate the issue."

"Okay." She nodded and smiled, all the while rolling the Quinton name around in her head until recognition dawned. When he turned away Suzan took her aside.

"He got Callee out of that drunk-and-disorderly last year. He's the best," she whispered, referring to a white-hot pop tart who had plowed through a tattoo shop storefront last year. The bratty star had avoided jail and simply cut a check for the damages, all the while regular Americans screamed *affluenza!* Quinton's involvement in her legal woes worried Steffi all of a sudden. How would it look for her to breeze through this incident as though she'd done nothing more sinister than jaywalk? Hell, her memory continued to fail her.

"You're lucky nobody was hurt, and that you only drove that limo fifty feet before you wrecked it." Suzan fished a filmy handkerchief from her purse. "I brought you the tops in representation, but stopping the social media, forget it. And then there's the regular media."

"Be honest with me, Suzan. How bad was I?" she asked. "I honestly don't remember shit."

The shadow crossing Suzan's face scared her. Steffi pictured herself topless and frothing like a mad dog on the red carpet, her picture shared across the world. *Oh, dear. At least I hope I kept my clothes on.*

"We'll talk when there's fewer ears." Suzan patted her hand.

Right. They walked toward the main doors of the police station. The sky had darkened, yet lights from several TV cameras shone through the glass doors. Steffi reared back like a spooked horse. "We're not going out that way," she said.

"There's no choice. Donald has a car out front, hon, and if we take another exit we'll have to walk farther and attract more attention." Suzan draped the soft fabric square over Steffi's head and fastened the ends at her chin. "We just need to push through the crowd and crawl in."

*Heh.* Five feet or five hundred, it still worked out as a walk of shame. Steffi Corden, one of the decade's most promising television actresses, dashing out of a police station following a humiliating display. Two cops stood just outside the doors to push back the crowd, which she eyeballed at about thirty people. Not huge compared to the press present for the awards, but thirty cameras broadcasting to thirty channels and websites, seen by hundreds of thousands of people, shared that many times on Facebook and Twitter...

Suzan sensed her hesitation. "Sweetie, they're not going away. Police won't let you live here, either. It's do or die."

Had Suzan always talked to her this way, like a mother to a small child? Until this point, she'd been a model client for the agent, heeding career advice and behaving for the public. Well, when one removed all outbursts that involved Dash...other than that, she was Mary Effin' Poppins.

Donald J. Quinton arrived at Suzan's side, placing a large hand on her shoulder. "Ladies, are we okay?"

Steffi looked past him a moment at the officers milling around the registration desk. Some glanced their way as though showing genuine interest in them, others kept their heads bowed over paperwork. She didn't see the same cop who had escorted her out.

"There's a woman named Marleen in the holding cell right now." Steffi nodded her head that way. "I assume she was picked up on soliciting, or also possession. We didn't broach the subject."

Donald and Suzan waited.

"Can you send a lawyer from your firm to defend her? I'll pay the bill. They'll just give her to some overworked public defender otherwise, and I'm thinking a firm lawyer might actually help her instead of moving on to the next hooker because his docket is stuffed."

The lawyer shifted in place, frowning. He recovered a second later with a shrug. "Uh, sure. I guess. I'll make a call tonight."

"Or now. When we're in the car. Whichever's good," Steffi said. Weird. Here she was, offering the guy's firm more money. Why should it matter his firm would defend a sex worker? They seemed to have no qualms standing up for somewhat lethal one-hit wonders.

"Thank you." Steffi nodded, faced the doors and took a deep breath. "All right. Once more into the breach."

\* \* \* \*

Barry took the 'nothing to see here' brush-off from venue security in stride. He wasn't Steffi's keeper, and powerless to help. *Time to watch out for number one.*

Once he managed to free himself of everything television awards, he found his car—unmolested and no tickets on the windshield—and took off for the nearest drive-thru. No high-falutin' media mogul-sponsored dinner party for the seat warmers, not even a voucher for a nearby taco joint to say thanks for giving up four hours of your life. Barry ordered a double hamburger combo, upsized for the large soda and onion rings, then went straight home to decompress.

Yeah, it cost an extra buck to go big, but after tonight he deserved a treat. Tomorrow, he'd take on a few more driving gigs than he scheduled in a typical day to make up for the dent in his checking account.

For all the time burned up getting dinner and settling on the couch, he managed to hit all the talk shows at the critical start time. *Kip James Live* had been taped in a venue not far from the award ceremony, and Barry turned up the volume to hear the affable, dark-suited host begin his monologue, which naturally focused on the entertainment event.

"First off, congrats to everybody at *Danse Macabre* for their near-sweep this year." Pause for applause, nodding in approval. "Yes, what an awesome show. I can't wait to see how they'll top an amazing debut season, but I have heard spoilers." There came a sincere look into the camera, then a pause for the joke. "In the next season, the Grim Reaper will be coming to claim what's left of Steffi Corden's career."

*Chicka-boom* went the drums. The studio exploded with laughter, and Kip soaked it in. Barry swallowed hard on a bite of hamburger, tempted to switch stations. The other late-night shows taped early, so he'd likely not find any Steffi-bashing there. Not that he was interested in monitoring for any.

"I feel for Steffi, though. It must be heartbreaking to lose the Best Actress award, and then find out your show is on the bubble for cancelation," Kip continued. "It got so bad she decided to try her Plan B, but unfortunately her audition to become a RydeAlong driver kinda backfired on her."

The show then cut to an amateur video of Steffi hijacking the limo, and the subsequent crash. "Holy crap, you guys," Barry muttered, and shut off the TV, disgusted. So much for Hollywood taking care of their own. He thought of his own aspirations, and wondered if he should cut his losses and go back to Florida. If these people didn't think twice about kicking a star while she was down, how would they treat a screenwriter?

Barry ate in silence, chewing slowly so as not to upset his stomach. He had arrived in Los Angeles shortly after earning his Bachelor's in English at the University of Florida, on the promise of giving himself five years to break into the industry. He'd spent the first three in film school getting a Masters in Professional Writing, completing two feature-length screenplays to accompany the one already on his laptop when he'd stepped off the bus. Year Four began two months ago, with nary a lead progressing him. Oh, he'd met with agents — gained one, lost him then garnered interest from his assistant who wanted to be an agent before she changed her mind and moved to Australia — but his every pitch fell like lead from the sky.

He applied for grants, internships, programs, any call that appeared legitimate for which he was qualified. He thought being Cuban on his mother's side might help in situations where studios encouraged minorities to inquire, but he never seemed to make the cut. His stories were well done, with believable characters and drama…just not enough to make a producer hop up on a table and shout, "*This!* I want to make *this* movie."

No explosions, no bare tits, nothing that could parlay into merchandise. He tried to write more commercial material, but also found that difficult to sell. With a little over a year and a half left to his promise, he realized he'd go home to regroup if nothing happened. Teach writing in college. At least his family offered support, albeit with reluctance He sensed their skepticism every time he called home.

*Shit.* Barry checked his phone, sagging with relief on seeing no texts. Maybe his parents hadn't watched the awards after all — they really weren't the type to follow Hollywood. His mother, for certain, would want to know how he ended up onstage with a woman twice his age pawing at him, and if Randi Marsh was at least baptized a Catholic.

It was close to midnight back home, anyway, so they were probably in bed.

His phone chirped. Scratch that. He groaned and checked the screen, pitching louder when he saw who'd paged him.

"No, no, no, *no!*" He thrashed against his couch and cried out, then looked at his phone again. Still there. Barry pressed his thumb on the RydeAlong icon alerting him to a fare request and swiped it away. He'd marked himself unable to drive tonight, and though he needed the money to make up for what he'd lost as a seat filler, he wasn't in the mood to cart strangers around the city this late.

He slurped down the rest of his soda and the icon popped up again. Swiped away. Again. Barry sighed. "I'm off the clock!" he shouted at his phone, and this time left the icon blinking. Whoever requested him for a ride would get the hint, he hoped, and find another driver.

Not a chance. This time the ping alerted him to a text from an unfamiliar number, routed through the RydeAlong site. Barry had opted for the special notification feature for passengers with special needs to give him advanced warning.

*Mr. Spahn, I hope you are able to accept my request this evening. I am prepared to pay extra for this unique circumstance*, read the first text. It intrigued Barry enough to not erase it. After a few seconds, a second one appeared.

*I must advise you discretion is an absolute must in this matter. Please call for more information, and only if you are prepared to accept.*

"The plot thickens." Barry guessed he'd been contacted by some celebrity's personal assistant. It wouldn't be the first time a public figure used RydeAlong—some did it to look hip, but Barry read the horror stories on a private message board created for local drivers. He knew which cheapskate stars neglected to tip, who threw up in which car after a drinking binge and who received oral attention in the backseat on the way to Canoga Park for a movie sneak preview. It's why he tended to take fares in other parts of the city, away from the studios. Often, he ferried a number of hopefuls to and from auditions, so he found it difficult to avoid the area.

The double burger churned in his gut. He needed a shower and had hoped to slip into his flannels, but the text glared up from his phone, the letters growing larger in his mind as he thought about the money.

When he had signed up as a representative of the RydeAlong brand he'd studied the policies. Anyone who used the phone app to book a ride paid in advance according to the mileage driven for the specific trip from pickup to drop-off, with an added fee for gas. The company set this up as a safety measure so people wouldn't think the drivers had lots of cash on them, making them easy robbery targets. RydeAlong took a cut of the fare, leaving the rest to the driver via direct bank deposit.

Tips, while not against the rules, weren't exactly encouraged for that reason. If a guy slipped Barry a fiver, he took it. It meant five boxes of spaghetti in his pantry, meals for two weeks — a month if he skipped lunches.

Thankfully, RydeAlong didn't monitor private messages from potential fares, so they'd miss this carrot dangling in front of him. Whoever sent this wasn't supposed to give out a phone number, per the company policies.

At the very least, he'd hear the person out. Barry sank deeper into the couch. Whatever Mister or Miss Unique Circumstance wanted, they better have the money to back up their request, otherwise he'd fall asleep here in his monkey suit. It wasn't due back for another two days, anyway.

He punched in the digits and a voice cut through the first ring.

"Mr. Spahn, thank you for responding to my text. My client is in need of transportation services from a competent driver capable of the utmost discretion." Male, whiskey-voiced, to the point. "I see of all the L.A.-area RydeAlong drivers you are top-ranked, so naturally I've come to you first."

"Thanks." He didn't consider it a feather in his cap, but Barry attributed his popularity among RydeAlong users to his flexibility. "To be honest, I only have the high score because I'm willing to drive places others won't go. I also speak two other languages, which helps."

"Good to know." Whiskey McCircumstances wasn't in the mood to make idle chit-chat, he saw. "What I have in mind, however, is a long-term arrangement to begin tonight.

Exclusive to my client. This means you would suspend your association with RydeAlong, but we are prepared to pay you fairly for however long you are needed."

"So…you want a chauffeur?" Did he have to get a special license for that? His mind tingled at the thought of a steady job. He already had one, though, that of failed screenwriter. He hated the idea, too, of giving up his top rank on RydeAlong if it threatened future fares.

"I don't get it. Why don't you just hire a professional driver instead of trolling a rideshare app?"

The man on the other end chuckled. Smooth, like in a bar about to charm a woman off her stool and into bed. "I had considered it, but time is of the essence and since RydeAlong provides detailed profiles of their contracted drivers, it made vetting a potential hire easier for me."

If only the hunt for screenwriters worked the same way.

"Mr. Spahn, are you able to meet me and my client in the next hour?"

"I have to tell you, sir, I just got back from a, uh, volunteer event. I'd like to shower and change before I think about doing anything."

"Understood. If you're close to our location it won't be an issue."

"Fair enough. Where am I headed?" He still needed to accept the pending fare on the app, so it wasn't a done deal yet.

Barry listened for instructions, focusing on the two words that caused his breath to still. *Police station*.

*This better be worth it.*

# Chapter Four

His intuition kicked in the second he rounded the corner and spotted the tall aerials reaching for the dimming sky. News programs logos covered the sides of vans and panel trucks, and onlookers mingled with reporters and cameramen to form a sizable, yet somewhat calm, mob lining the entrance to the Hollywood Community Police Station.

This summons to escort a few passengers away from this building had nothing to do with Ms. Corden's wild ride from earlier, or did it? He'd come to pick up another badly behaving starlet. Maybe one of those socialite twins who majored in duck-face selfies.

Doubtful. *Damn, what are the odds?* How many times would Steffi Corden thwart his writing schedule this week? And had his agreement to this fare counted as acceptance for the long-term part? *Oh, hell.*

He hoped Whiskey Voice was riding along. They were going to have a nice talk on the drive home.

His instructions were to pull alongside the curb as close to the front doors as possible—a Herculean task given the bodies and vehicles occupying so much of the road. He edged through, however, and the purr of his VW Jetta proved important enough to encourage people to give him berth. He garnered several curious stares but he fixed his gaze straight ahead until he settled on a spot just kissing the bumper of a black sedan.

Somebody must have seen the RydeAlong magnet he kept on the fuel door. A lady tapped on his window and shouted, "Are you here to pick up Steffi Corden? Do you know when police expect to release her?"

The man he had talked to earlier, who had identified himself as Mr. Quinton while giving directions, had warned him of obstacles. He'd never implied a crush of people to rival the waiting line for the latest iThingie, or reporters asking him questions. *Terrific, here come the cameras. I'm going to be on TV again, huh?* He still hadn't checked to see how he had looked during Steffi's mic drop at the awards, and imagined that was damaging enough to the career he had yet to launch.

He'd had the foresight to throw a hoodie over his T-shirt. He pulled the ash-gray cover loosely on top of his hair and bent over the steering wheel, calling out, "No comment," while the clock ticked.

*Heh, some magic words.* The reporter stayed put. "Do you know if Steffi Corden's been charged with anything?"

"No comment."

"Is she being released into somebody's custody or leaving on her own?"

"What did I just say?" Barry shouted at the woman leaning on his car, and she took a step back, her eyes wide. "I don't know a freaking thing. I'm just the damn driver."

*Finally.* The woman skittered away and Barry let in a deep breath, but he soon saw why he'd lost her attention. The front doors of the building opened and three figures pushed out, a tall dark man and a shorter woman framing the third, who held a hand to her face as a shield.

He recognized the dress. It had lost its luster from earlier in the day. Damn shame, since she'd looked so pretty.

So, he now worked for Steffi Corden, or her lawyer... he still wasn't sure. At the very least, couldn't one of her handlers there have brought her a change of clothes? The walk of shame with the added scorched glam factor made her appear all the more pathetic.

"Steffi! Steffi!" Voices called questions to her but he tuned out the press. He turned on his radio and let Guns N' Roses blow away the chaos surrounding him. The crowd waylaid his passengers—he could afford two minutes of classic rock to decompress.

The man—Mr. Quinton, Barry presumed—held up one hand as though to will away the throng. When they reached the car, Barry killed the radio and unlocked the door. "We have no comment," the man called out, halfway into the front passenger seat. "My client wishes for privacy at this time. Thank you for understanding."

The client in question dove into the back and slammed against her door with a loud sigh. "Holy crap, that crowd's bigger than I thought. Has all of L.A. come to watch me crash and burn?" Steffi gave off a stench he had trouble naming. A tinge of alcohol mixed with disinfectant, if he had to guess.

"Honey, they already saw the crash. In time, they'll forget about it," said her female companion. "Now, buckle up. We still have to get through this crowd."

"Forget? It's probably all over the Internet, the news..." Steffi glanced up, and Barry met her eyes in the rearview mirror. "Oh, *hai*, Mr. Driver. I'm Steffi Corden. You probably remember me from a failed streaming site drama and the hot mess I created on live TV earlier."

Not a single glint of recognition in her eyes. He couldn't decide whether to feel relieved or insulted. Was he that unmemorable?

"Stef, that's enough."

"Suze, I don't care." After some dramatic huffing, she pressed her nose against the window and dragged it over the glass. Barry winced at the piggy face she made, that media cameras no doubt captured for tomorrow's wires.

Mr. Quinton managed to close the passenger door on the rest of the reporters but didn't buckle up. "Drive," he ordered.

Barry put the car into reverse and backed up a few inches before easing forward to miss the car in front of him. He tapped the gas pedal, urging the sea of busybodies to either side of them and out of their path. "Where to? The app didn't send a destination address." The request had denoted the police station as the pickup and end—it was viewed as a red flag sometimes for RydeAlong drivers, but Barry had slipped down this rabbit hole some time ago.

"Away from here, as quickly as possible without rolling over anybody. Drive around a bit." Mr. Quinton twirled his finger in the universal symbol for 'whatever works'. *Fair enough*. After a few months contracting with RydeAlong, he knew the city well. He'd hop on Santa Monica Boulevard and take a casual tour down Sunset. He guessed his party would frown upon him stopping at the next quickie mart to pick up moist wipes to clean the window Steffi now soiled.

"Where're we going?" Steffi demanded, sounding like a petulant child. Nobody seemed to find it endearing.

Mr. Quinton turned to regard her. "Ms. Corden, you're in a safe space now. All you need to do is relax. Suzan and I are handling everything."

"I wanna go home."

Barry sensed something this time in the way Steffi spoke. Less like a spoiled brat, more like somebody about to break down in a blubbering, vomity mess. He recognized the tone in many a plastered passenger calling RydeAlong to deliver them from self-inflicted, rum-soaked evil.

He cleared his throat. His job was to drive and not ask questions, but this was still his Jetta and he prided himself on a car often ranked as 'super clean' by RydeAlong clientele. When the lawyer turned to him he asked, "Do you think we should stop for coffee…or something?" As much as he hated the idea of drinks in his car, he didn't know if the attorney or the lady had something else in mind to calm down Steffi, like a syringe of knockout drugs.

"She will be fine, thank you. Ms. Corden lives in the Hills, but we don't wish to head straight there. I'm sure we'll see a few vultures prowling around the house, but I'd like to have her lay low for a while."

"Okay." Their money to burn. Barry wasn't sure how a joy ride down the Sunset Strip stood to dispel interest in a drunk starlet, but Mr. Quinton acted as though he'd dealt with this sort of thing before. The idea of replaying the O.J. Simpson drive left a sour taste in his mouth, so he'd stay off the freeway.

Driving calmed him—it was one reason he took the RydeAlong work when he wasn't writing—so he hoped the movement had a similar effect on Steffi.

Steffi continued to mutter about wanting to go home and fall into bed. Barry checked on her through the rearview mirror when he could, at stoplights and long pauses at corners. The woman she called Suze patted her hand and tried to get Steffi to look her in the eye. He tried to discern their relationship as he drove—personal assistant, concerned relative, manager, perhaps all of the above. He didn't get the impression Suze coddled her, though. The advice came in curt snips, and it did not sound placating.

"We need to think about damage control," Suze was saying. "Craft an apology for a public statement, decide where and when to deliver it—"

"You can't just put out a press release?" Steffi broke in. "Or I could tweet it... Where's my purse?"

"Donald has it in his briefcase for safekeeping. Steffi, please, let's focus." Suze brought out her phone. Barry wondered at the post-awards activity, and how Steffi had trended as a result of her embarrassing stunt.

Then his veins ran cold, and his fingers numbed on the steering wheel. If Suze pulled up video of Steffi crashing Gabby's speech, would she see him in the background? What could she do about it, aside from asking to be let out of the car, and why do that? He sat here now, well-aware of Steffi's inebriation and the need for discretion. If anything, his attempt to escort her offstage gave him an advantage at this job.

On Sunset Boulevard he drove past familiar landmarks. He caught site of a fast-food joint and his stomach rumbled. He remembered the remainder of the In-N-Out meal he'd left at home and wished he had finished eating it. He figured he'd drive as far as the Roxy Theatre before U-turning for the Hills area. Plenty of time to distance Steffi from the media, and he hoped to receive a decent tip from these people to keep his mouth shut.

Mr. Quinton leaned close, forcing Barry to shift his attention to the front of the car. "Mr. Spahn, when do you believe we'll arrive in the general vicinity of Ms. Corden's home?"

"We're talking the Hills?" Barry tapped at the GPS mounted on his windshield, where he kept stored a few regular addresses. One lady he ferried several times a month lived at the base of the popular residential area — widow, always wore mismatched colors and trowel-applied makeup, loved to talk about her cats. "Barring traffic, no longer than half an hour."

"That's fine." Mr. Quinton gave him Steffi's address and he plugged it into the device. "After we arrive, I'll wish to speak to you privately about our arrangement."

"Sure." Barry wanted to laugh at the shifting moods within this confined, rolling space. The lawyer spoke all cloak and dagger while checking the mirrors for trailing paparazzi. The backseat reeked of reality TV drama with the sobbing diva and no-nonsense handler. It'd make a great scene in a script about the Hollywood life, if he could get home to write it.

A minute passed in blessed silence and Barry started to relax. The serenity soon died, though, when something slid across the back of his neck and his skin prickled. Steffi's fingers touched his collar, tugging at the fuzzy tufts of hair he'd neglected to have sheared off because it'd been forever since he last visited a barber. Given the choice between vanity and food, he always picked the latter.

Steffi's voice slipped into his ear with more silk than Randi Marsh's had. She leaned forward, her face pressed on his headrest. "I know you from somewhere," she purred.

His heart throbbed. *Terrific*. Despite the whiskey haze wafting from her general direction, and the alleged gaps in her memory, she had recognized him at last. She'd realized he was the asshole who attempted to thwart her revenge on Gabby Randall-Gregory, and she'd pitch holy hell, no doubt, until he pulled over and let her loose.

All in his imagination, anyway. Her hand rubbing his shoulder unnerved him, as though she might suddenly Vulcan neck pinch him until he crashed.

"*Modern Family*, right?" she asked. "You were in that episode with those guys, when they got trapped in that department store. I thought I saw you."

"That hardly narrows it down," Suze said. Movement from the back alluded to the other woman trying to pull Steffi back.

"I'm sorry, it wasn't me," Barry said. "I'm actually not an actor."

"No?" Steffi hiccupped, then belched. "Well, you're a wannabe in the industry, right? I mean, why else would you cart strangers around in your car, where people stink up your seats and pick at loose threads on the upholstery. It's not exactly a career ambition."

"Ms. Corden," Mr. Quinton — Donald — warned her with a sharp look.

"To be honest, I've dreamed of doing nothing else," Barry said, his lip quirking up at his joke. He could mention his screenwriting in front of the lawyer, the actress and Suze the professional whatever, but why? Once bitten on that scenario, when he'd talked of progress on a script to a director at a coffee shop, only to be accused of harassment. "First thing I did when I got off the bus was lease this car and sign up to drive. This gig is a masochist's dream."

"You're funny." Steffi cackled and settled into her seat, while Barry tucked that line into his mental back burner for later use. After a few seconds Steffi's snickering turned to snuffling, then a steady low roar. A glimpse in the mirror confirmed she'd passed out with her mouth agape, head lolling by the window.

"Thank God," Suze murmured. Donald rubbed the bridge

of his nose. Everything remained silent for the remainder of the drive, save for the voices in Barry's head trying out dialogue he'd never be able to repeat in a story.

Steffi's lawyer insisted on discretion. No compliance, no supplemental pay. Besides, this brief time spent with Steffi's handlers had him wondering if they worked for her best interests. She didn't need another person taking advantage of her by dramatizing her downfall in hopes of getting it optioned.

"Turn here. It's the pale yellow house with the red Spanish tile roof. Next to the bigger one." Suze's finger came into his peripheral view and he steered the car according to her directions. The GPS continued to track the drive, but Barry's eyes fixed on the eclectic string of homes lining the street. From this view, as the car puttered up the incline, he saw nothing spectacular—the houses were landscaped with lush plants and the paint bright and smooth, yes—but he imagined once you stepped inside any one of them you'd find a magnificent view of the city on the other end, perhaps a luxury pool or an outdoor fire pit relaxation area that cost as much as his car.

If any paparazzi lurked around Steffi's home—one of the more modest buildings on the block with a limestone pathway leading to the arched front door and a garage that appeared sunken into the hill—they hid well. Rambo well. Barry pulled into the driveway and checked an adjacent bush for eyes.

"Suzan, is there a car inside?" Donald opened his briefcase and pulled out a set of keys with a flower-shaped fob. "I'd prefer not to have Mr. Spahn's car visible in case we have 'visitors'."

Barry doubted anybody would care about a car sitting in the drive, but he considered Steffi's current state and understood somebody would have to assist in walking her limp body a la *Weekend at Bernie's* to the front door. That wouldn't come off as flattering shared on a million Facebook pages.

"Push the center of the daisy. It opens the garage," Suzan said. The *zip* and *clunk* when she released her seatbelt set Barry's teeth on edge.

The wide, windowless door ratcheted slowly upward, revealing a pair of hipster-type bicycles leaning inside against the left wall and a refrigerator by the door leading into the house. Beach chairs hanging from hooks, a large cooler under a workbench and a sack of potting soil in the far corner completed the list of non-automotive objects one would find in a garage. No car filling the space. Not his business to ask.

They waited for the door to close before exiting. Barry moved to open Steffi's door but Suzan had rounded the car with great speed and hip-checked him. "I got her. She needs to get some sleep. Why don't you and Donald...take care of business?"

Suzan dipped back into the car long enough to retrieve a groggy Steffi, who regarded her garage through eye slits. "The hell are we? I wanna go home."

"You *are* home, dear." Suzan hooked an arm around her waist and pulled her to the side entrance.

"Where's my car?"

"Where you left it, at Marva's." The woman let out a heavy sigh. "Crap. Marva's probably wondering why we haven't showed up yet."

"Does this Marva have the Internet? She knows," Donald cracked.

Suzan shook her head, and didn't respond to the man's sarcasm. "Let's get into you PJs and into bed, sweetheart. Gentlemen, you can use the living room for your business. I'll stay with her for the rest of the night. She doesn't have domestic help."

Barry watched, feeling as though he hovered on the perimeter of a TV drama without permission to intercede. Curiosity burned his mind and he feared if he asked a question or moved to assist either one of these people would snap back. They gave him the impression he was here on a need-to-know basis, but hearing about this Marva person, who had Steffi's car, brought more mystery into the evening.

Best as he could guess, Steffi had driven to another assistant's house to prepare for the awards and had taken a car from there to the venue. That being the case, why drive her straight home? Suzan could have driven Steffi's car to the house.

"Man. This is nuts."

"I hear you," Donald said, and Barry turned hot. He hadn't meant to say anything out loud, but with the women in the house it relieved some of the anxiety. Donald gestured toward the entrance with a placating smile and assured him everything would soon make sense.

"Everything must seem odd to you, Mr. Spahn. I'll be honest, I've been practicing law in Los Angeles for fifteen years, worked with a number of public figures, and every day I think I've seen just about everything."

"I'd think dealing with a drunk actress showing her ass on live TV registers low on the cuckoo scale," Barry said, then when Donald frowned, "metaphorically, that is. If Steffi actually mooned anybody, I didn't see it."

"I understand, and you probably want to get home for the night so let's get down to business." They entered Steffi's house and Barry marveled at the modest décor. As with the exterior, the homeowner kept to the quaint Spanish motif with a kitchen done in warm shades of orange and yellow with painted tiled countertops. Religious iconography, shining wood and solemn saints, decorated the walls, and as they passed into the great room he spotted a bold painting over a white sofa, that of blinding yellow sunflowers against a blue sky.

*Ah, how the other half lives.* He liked this place. Luxurious yet still cozy, reminiscent of a style his mother would adore. Donald took a seat on the sofa and unlatched his briefcase on the coffee table but Barry executed a slow turn to see the whole room. Large sliding doors exposed a beautiful courtyard ringed with wicker furniture surrounding a fire pit, overlooking twinkling La-La Land. Steffi had party lights strung along the eaves of the house and around a tree bordering the cliffside.

He then panned his gaze across to the wall opposite the sofa, which faced the fireplace. Above the mantel... Holy cow.

"Is that an original Frida Kahlo?" he asked after catching his breath.

Donald studied the painting for a second. "If it is, I hope it's insured." He shuffled some papers. "If you'll have a seat..."

He settled into the chair next to Donald and watched the man's fingers twine. Donald wore a gigantic class ring with a smooth onyx stone. From where he sat, he couldn't miss *YALE* engraved on the side. "Before we go any further, I'd like for you to read over this non-disclosure agreement. I've been charged to act as Ms. Corden's counsel, and in this capacity, I intend to protect her privacy to the best of my ability. If you feel you're unwilling or unable to cooperate this discussion ends and I'll give you the extra compensation I mentioned in our phone conversation, in cash." To show he meant business, Donald produced his wallet and pulled out a few hundred-dollar bills.

Spaghetti dinners for a year—with jarred tomato sauce instead of ketchup packets, even.

Barry took the sheet of paper and glanced at the text. A standard contract—from what he read, Steffi's team wanted his assurance that he wouldn't run to TMZ or whoever the second he left the house and cash in on his experience. The awards fiasco had given the media enough gold, and Barry shouldn't have been bothered by a simple contract. However...

"Do I at least get to know my role in all of this, before I commit to anything?" he asked. "You contacted me initially for my driving skills and high RydeAlong rating, so I'm guessing you want me on call for another trip? You don't need to give me an agreement for that. I signed plenty of stuff with the company already."

Donald nodded. "Ms. Corden will require a driver for the foreseeable future. At least sixty days."

Barry envisioned a puzzle piece sliding into place, forming a clearer picture of Steffi's predicament. Her spur-of-the-moment joyride had cost her a driver's license. He'd be the Morgan Freeman to her Jessica Tandy for as long as it remained revoked.

"Will I get to take other fares while I'm contracted to this gig? If Steffi chooses not to go out for a week, I lose money."

"To answer both, you can't...and you won't, Mr. Spahn."

"Barry, please. I'm not a formal guy."

Donald chuckled. "We are prepared to pay you well above minimum wage based on the forty-hour work week."

So, a job-job. Something he vowed never to resort to, unless he got hired to a TV series to write.

On the other hand, this lasted only two months. He might gain some perspective about the industry, and if he drove her to a meeting or audition he might find a foot in the door himself.

*What the hell*. He'd known aspiring actors who'd signed away their dignity for a lot less. He set the contract on the coffee table and asked for a pen.

That out of the way, Donald resumed his lawyer voice, "Mr. Spahn, as I gathered from your earlier comments, you're aware of the legal trouble Ms. Corden faces. She's been under a fair amount of strain of late thanks to negative press and concerns over her job. All of this emotion, unfortunately, came to a head tonight."

Barry nodded. An idea for an attorney character formed in his mind as he listened.

"Without going into the boring details, I managed a deal to Ms. Corden's benefit. She will not have to appear in court, she will not be formally charged with a crime, but she doesn't get away scot-free."

"The license deal."

"That, and Ms. Corden will record public service announcements for the HPD warning against intoxicated driving, and commit to ten hours of community service."

Barry wondered if Steffi knew all that yet. In the blink of an eye, he saw himself driving her not to Ron Howard's office to discuss a lead role in his next film, but to an exit ramp off the freeway and leaving her there to pick up garbage. *Fuck.*

"Doesn't seem like a lot," he said.

Donald turned up his palms. "She hasn't been charged with a crime."

*Right.* "I take it this is an as-needed position, meaning I come when summoned."

"I'll let you work out the particulars with Ms. Corden. My job is simply to clear her legal troubles and ensure she holds up her end of the bargain I made for her," Donald spoke without humor and filed Barry's signed form into a briefcase pocket. "As she's in Ms. Carey's capable hands at the moment, it appears we are free to leave. I expect either woman will be in touch with you tomorrow."

"Not a problem. I have the address on my GPS, so I'm set." After an awkward pause and another, longing stare out the glass doors, he asked Donald if he required a ride out of the Hills. It unnerved him a bit that neither he nor Suzan mentioned his presence at the awards. Perhaps the lawyer hadn't seen the footage yet.

When Donald did, would it cost him this job?

"If you don't mind." Donald handed him the cash bonus promised him and asked for a lift back to the police station where he'd left his car. "You can drive directly there this time," he added.

"Will do." Barry pocketed the bills, thinking he'd set a few dollars aside and put a bag of frozen meatballs on his growing grocery list.

# Chapter Five

Sometime between the moment she'd dozed off in the back of some dude's car and when she'd landed home in bed, a troupe of bongo players had taken up residence inside her head. They tapped a steady but light tattoo throughout a surreal dream involving Steffi trapped in an airplane with two dozen people holding Best Actress trophies. Halfway into the flight, somebody nudged her to stand and serve everybody drinks.

*Ugh.* Even in unconsciousness, she swore never to tip back a cocktail again. She swallowed cotton as she slept.

The gradual, cacophonous drum circle throbbing in her ears finally roused her from her near coma around eleven a.m., so said her bedside clock. The heavy curtains blocking her sliding balcony door kept away the natural light, which suited her fine. The dimness allowed her vision to adjust without discomfort, and she rose to a sitting position in bed. Somebody—Suzan, she hoped—had gotten her out of her gown and constricting underthings and into a billowy sleep shirt.

"Suzan?" *Ugh.* Drier than the California desert. She craved water. Then coffee, like what she smelled wafting in from the kitchen. Along with voices, both high-pitched. Steffi guessed female and thought about who else besides Suzan had come to watch the aftermath of her downward spiral into career oblivion.

*Not Mom. Please, Lord.* No, not possible. Regina Corden lived in London now with Number Four, an elderly playwright of forgettable family dramas. Assuming she'd stayed up until the wee hours and learned of her daughter's disgrace, Regina couldn't fly into L.A. that quickly.

*Gabby then? Why her?* The voices down the hall bantered and laughed, their words undistinguishable to Steffi's ears. Gabby was too nice a person to come and gloat, or storm into her house to demand an apology. She wouldn't be surprised to turn on the TV and see a video byte of her rival making excuses for Steffi, trying to diffuse the situation.

*Gag.*

She tested her feet on the carpet and, when the dizziness didn't overcome her, padded to the kitchen. The coffee aroma strengthened and all senses snapped alert. She knew with one sniff which blend Suzan, or whoever, had set to brew and her mouth watered for a shot.

Suzan, still in last night's clothes, sat at the breakfast table with Eileen Chester, Steffi's friend and an executive at ExStream. They continued to chat, focused on each other, as Steffi opened a cabinet without making noise and reached for a mug. Their conversation broke the second she lifted the carafe from the warmer.

Eileen clutched her mug with both hands, fingers twined through the handle, and looked up with a gasp. "Hey, sweetie. How're you feeling? I brought Winchell's." She pointed to a yellow rectangular box near the sink. Steffi dragged her tongue over her top row of teeth, imagining the enamel dissolving with the first bite of donut.

For a brief moment, she feared opening the box. Eileen's tone smacked of sympathy and warning of bad news to come. If she raised that lid and found her every favorite variety of sweet dough—the glazed French, the chocolate iced Buttermilk Bar, the lemon filled with sugar—she'd probably start crying.

"Steffi?" Suzan turned in her chair, frowning. "Are you okay?"

She poured the coffee and lingered by the box. "You guys, I'm an adult. Whatever bad news these donuts are supposed to soften, just give it to me. I can take it." She tipped up the lid, like ripping off a bandage. Half glazed, half chocolate-covered cake. "You didn't put much thought into this, did you, Eileen?"

"Sorry. There was a line."

"There's always a line at Winchell's."

"I wanted to be here when you got up, and some jerk ahead of me cleaned them out of French style." Eileen rose and moved to give a hug, which Steffi didn't shrug off. She focused on the donuts, her hand hovering between the two flavor choices, otherwise she'd become so lost in her friend's embrace she might process last night and start crying.

"I was just telling Eileen about Donald, and our current plans," Suzan said as the women took their seats around the table. Steffi had one of each donut on a napkin and she tore the glazed ring in half. She shook a flake of sugar into her coffee before dunking the end.

"Okay. So, I'm not being charged with any wrongdoing, right? No court or jail, nothing bad?" Good news, for once. "I can go back to work."

Eileen cleared her throat, her head down. "Steffi, I think you're aware this was coming, well before the awards. ExStream has decided not renew your show."

The bite of coffee-soaked donut slid down hard and landed in her gut like a lead ball. The idea of there being no such thing as bad publicity, it appeared, amounted to zilch.

"This is my fault. I embarrassed the network with my speech."

"It's a great show, Steffi. An awesome show," Eileen said. "Y'all earned the nominations you got." She shrugged and sighed. "The numbers weren't there to support it and this decision was set before…all that."

"Well, if you're comparing us to *Danse Macabre*, it makes sense," Steffi groused.

"You can't compare the two, Steffi." This from Suzan. "Their success doesn't compound the failure of *ViP*. It sucks that ExStream isn't willing to hang on for a while to see if fortunes turn around" — Steffi didn't miss her agent's sharp glare at Eileen — "but you shouldn't take this personally."

"Have you talked to Elliot? ExStream isn't the only game in town." Steffi could count on both hands shows canceled by the Big Three that had found new life on streaming networks. Plural. ExStream had competitors, so why weren't the producers shopping *ViP* to potential new homes?

"Steffi," Suzan began.

"I want you two to stop it. Stop talking in that voice like you're about to tell me my cat's dead."

"Fine." Her agent huffed. "Elliot wanted me to pass along to you that he's going to concentrate on a new project."

"What?" Elliot Voller had developed the series two years ago with her in mind as the lead, and acted as her head cheerleader. He wrote or co-wrote every episode and often consulted with her on character quirks and motivation. On the night the show had launched he'd arranged to have congratulatory telegrams sent from three former Vice Presidents, all of which she had framed. He saw to minor things, too, like flowers in her trailer and her favorite coffee at the craft table, just to ensure her a pleasant work experience.

Reading Suzan's face, and knowing Elliot hadn't the balls to break his news in person, made her feel all the more like a wicked witch. What had she done to alienate his generosity?

Besides get drunk and make a damn fool of herself on live TV?

Eileen cleared her throat again, capturing Steffi's attention. Her hunched posture and slackened features made it clear she had no desire to listen in on an argument that didn't impact her. "Steffi, I hope you won't feel as though we're dumping on you here. *ViP* isn't the only show we haven't ordered more episodes for. The higher-ups simply decided their eyes were bigger than their stomachs, so to speak. Too many shows saturated the programming schedule for original works, forcing some cuts."

"ExStream is losing money on the original programs, is

what you're saying."

Eileen nodded. She tensed. Steffi imagined this affected her friend's job, and she wondered if Eileen shouldered any blame for not effectively marketing *ViP* and other cut shows.

"I understand ExStream put in an order for three more seasons of *Danse Macabre*," Steffi said, guessing that's where budget that otherwise would have gone to *ViP* Season Two went.

"It's a monster hit, Steffi. Of course, they're negotiating longer contracts with Too True so another channel doesn't horn in. They're counting on *Danse* to increase subscriptions and get them out of the hole."

Steffi side-eyed her agent. "Are you guys working with Elliot on his new series, too?"

"I'm not at liberty to say." Eileen's attention turned to points around her. She pushed away her mug, grabbed her purse to fish through the contents and glanced at the donuts as though contemplating one for the road. Eyes darted left and right, up and down, everywhere but fixed on her.

Eileen chose to say nothing, but Steffi got her answer, anyway.

"I have to go, hon. Meetings today. You know how it is." Eileen stood to leave and did her the courtesy of bringing her mug to the sink. "I'll call you later, okay? We'll get some sushi."

Steffi followed suit and drew her friend into a tight hug. She wanted to—with her ties to ExStream severed, who knew when the two would meet up again? Steffi got the impression she'd become *persona non grata* there and therefore spur Eileen's reluctance to hang out. "That sounds great. Text me." Eileen wouldn't, not in the near future.

When the woman left Steffi grabbed a third donut from the box and stacked it with the others she hadn't finished. *How about I finish the whole damn dozen, slip into a sugar coma?* It wasn't as if she had work to look forward to.

Suzan busied herself with her phone for a moment,

tapping and scrolling. Finally, Steffi broke the silence. "Am I a bad client?"

"What? Of course not!" Suzan's eyebrows raised nearly to her hairline. "Why ask such a thing?"

She picked off a chunk of the cake donut and bit into the chocolate glaze. More sugar than cocoa coated her tongue, but she welcomed the indulgence. "Everything I did last night, you know it wasn't spontaneous."

"So you planned to interrupt Gabby in the middle of her acceptance speech and then hijack a car in a drunken hissy fit, is that right? You know all I ask is for you to run these crazy schemes past me before you put them into motion."

Steffi wanted to head-table right there. It meant moving the donuts, and she lacked the energy. "I'd been in a bad mood all year, when I wasn't working. Gabby and Dash got back together and enjoyed all this good press, some of it at my expense. I was a fricking powder keg and somebody lit the match."

Suzan set down her phone and folded her arms, listening.

"People who watched *ViP* seemed to like the show, but always had nits to pick. Either the cast wasn't diverse enough, or too diverse, or my character was too stupid to live." She shook her head. "I'm only the actor, and I read the scripts they gave me. Even when I offered suggestions to people they nodded and did their own thing, except for Elliott sometimes. Then the night of the awards I go and read how cancelation is inevitable and I'm to blame."

"Where did you read that?"

Steffi snatched Suzan's phone and waved the screen at her. "Just Google my name. Every wannabe pundit has an opinion on my career."

"They all have assholes, too. Doesn't mean they're right." Suzan took back her phone and blacked out the screen.

Steffi dunked the rest of the glazed donut and wolfed it. *Slow down, girl, save the rest for dinner.* And tomorrow's meals, too. No work meant rationing what she had until the next role. Could be days, weeks... Lord forbid longer than that. She earned residuals on some past work, but that money only went so far after bills and taxes.

"You want to know what I think?"

Steffi waited for Suzan to answer. The agent sipped her coffee and drummed her nails once over the mug.

"Elliot has a thing for you. Had, rather. You remember I wasn't all that keen on you signing on to *ViP* because I wasn't certain it was the right path for your career."

"Yes, and I argued with you because lots of A-listers have shows with streaming networks. Oscar winners."

"Established actors, Steffi," Suzan pointed out. "I'm not saying you're not a household name, but your star's still on the rise." At least the woman said it with confidence. Steffi doubted she'd weather this slump. "I know you wanted a marquee project, and despite the award nominations I still don't think *ViP* was it."

"I guess your wish came true," Steffi mumbled.

"I take no pleasure in the show's demise. I'm rooting for you here." Suzan clutched her hand and tugged in a silent order to lift her gaze. "I maintain Elliot brought you in because he was sexually attracted to you. Your moping over Dash Gregory when he suddenly became hot again obviously turned him off. He's not going to invest another second in you because he's moved on to the next starlet he wants to poke."

Steffi considered her agent's theory and saw some truth in it. It wouldn't have been her first exposure to the casting couch. During one of her first auditions—for a flippin' toothpaste commercial—the director had wanted to see her breasts. She had questioned what her tits had to do with selling brighter smiles, and the guy had shown her the door. Had she let that experience color her perception of Hollywood, she might have boarded the first plane back to New York and followed in her mother's footsteps, acting on stage and avoiding other media. Regina had hoped to see her daughter pursue another profession, but she still offered her best wishes…and little else.

Steffi didn't benefit from being the daughter of one of Broadway's grand dames. After a producer, adapting a play to film, had passed over Regina in the lead role she had originated on stage for a 'more bankable' actress, the elder Corden had eschewed film and TV altogether, save for the Tony Awards. Everything Steffi had accomplished, it had happened on her own.

Well, with Suzan's help.

"What now, Suzan?" She swept up donut crumbs and icing bits onto her plate and started to clear the table.

"What else, but damage control? I'm going back to my office to write up an official statement that will serve as your apology to Gabby and Too True, and to the academy. Then I'll start calling any and all producers who are least likely to hang up the second I mention your name." Suzan pocketed her phone and smoothed the wrinkles in her skirt. It took Steffi a moment to realize her agent wore the same outfit from when they had gotten her out of jail.

"You stayed over?" Man, she'd been so out of it.

"Yeah, and I don't have a car. Yours is still with Marva, and there's no rush in retrieving it since your license has been suspended."

"Wait, in the what with who now?"

Suzan rolled her eyes her and by rote recapped the punishment handed down from the Hollywood Police Department, the deal her smooth-as-silk lawyer buddy had brokered. Two months away from the wheel, a few finger-wagging ads and community service.

"Ah, fuck, am I gonna have to pick up used condoms on the beach or some crap like that?" This morning required more coffee.

"We'll figure it out. It's only ten hours. At worst, we'll visit some high schools and you give a 'just say no' speech. Or a weekend shift at a homeless shelter spooning gravy over chicken."

"Jeez a Lou. I'll just pick up the damn rubbers."

Suzan settled her with a placating wave to sit again.

"I'll find you something painless. I paged that RydeAlong driver Donald hired while Eileen was here, and he'll be at the house any minute. I need to borrow him to get home," she said. "He's working exclusively for you until you're cleared to drive again."

"How much are *we* paying this dude?" She blanched at the number Suzan gave her. "Damn it, lady. I just lost my job."

Suzan nodded, placating her. "We will budget for him, okay? It's only for two months, so you cut back on a few things for a while, or we find you a quick commercial to tide you over. Point is, when you're ready you'll need a ride and he's there, but don't go too crazy."

Translation: no more joy rides. Don't be a bitch, at least not in public.

"Gotcha. Trip to the grocery store, good. Tijuana, bad."

Suzan glared at her, but only for a moment as the sound of an engine filled the background. "I bet that's him. I think after he drops me off, I'll send him home. You ought to stay in today. Give it some time for all this to blow over before you go out—"

"There's no food in the house, other than the donuts," Steffi protested. No point in taking inventory—she lived hand-to-fast-food sack, regardless of her financial state.

"Place an order online with your grocer and he'll pick it up then." Suzan rolled her eyes, ever the exasperated guardian. "It's not that complicated."

"It is when you can't find your phone." Steffi whipped her head right to left. She'd had the landline disconnected to dissuade cranks and stalkers. "Please tell me we didn't leave my purse at the theater."

"I told you Donald grabbed it for you last night at the station. I'm sure it's around. You'll live." The sound of Suzan's phone interrupted the argument, and the agent gasped on looking at the number.

"Holy cow," she said. "It's Gabby Randall."

While the agreement with Steffi's people stipulated he'd drive only for her and others within her inner circle as needed, Barry found it difficult to turn away a longtime passenger who tipped well. He tried to explain the situation to Helen Knox, a character actress hired often for sassy senior citizen roles in sitcoms, but she had to get to Burbank early for a table reading and, skating close to ninety and unable to drive herself, wanted her best fella to take her.

He'd been up since six, transferring the demons in his head to metaphorical paper. He banged out three scenes of a new work in progress when the request came through the RydeAlong app, and he cursed when he realized he had forgotten to suspend his profile. *Ah, well.* He figured Steffi continued to sleep off her stint in the joint and so he picked up Helen in the lobby of her retirement villa.

He wouldn't tell if Helen wouldn't.

"What're doing this week?" He set the radio to the conservative talk station she enjoyed and kept the volume low.

"It's that show with the nerds, you know the one. They're all socially inept yet manage to get laid every few episodes." Helen rooted through her purse for her reading glasses. "So one of them is at a drugstore for last-minute condoms and tries to cut in line, and I slut-shame him and give him hell. Same old bullshit I've done on a dozen shows already."

Barry had to hand it to his favorite fare. He admired her lack of filter. "Why do you keep taking these parts if you don't like them? It's like every time I've driven you into Burbank for the last two years you've waited in line at a drugstore, at the movies, at some nondescript electronics store..."

"Tell me about it. What I wouldn't give to wait in line at a strip club for once. Or anything on that *Danse Macabre*." Helen grinned, showing straight teeth much younger than her years. "That gorgeous Reaper can hump *me* into the afterlife, boy howdy."

Barry nearly ran a stop sign, laughing so hard. He recovered to avoid an oncoming car and waited to catch his breath.

"Helen, you're killing me."

She gave him a sly smile. "You see that show win all the awards last night?"

"Up close and personal. I got roped into a seat-filler gig, and never again."

"I know, dear." Helen had her phone out now, playing a clip of Steffi barging in on Gabby's time. "You look great in a tux, by the way."

"Oh, crap." He kept his eyes on the road — he preferred that view over bad memories. "I really hope that blows over soon. Before you ask, I don't want to talk about it."

"Honey, I can imagine what happened. You got caught up in the action. Plus, Randi Marsh sank her talons into you good."

"I'm still bruised. Got these half-moon indentations all up my arm."

"Get you some of that beeswax ointment with menthol," Helen said and propped her elbow against the car window. "You still writing?"

"Every day." As he said it, though, the thought he might not get much done while driving for Steffi Corden spiked his fear. Donald Quinton had been reluctant to discuss downtime, and while Barry figured he was free to write when not driving he wondered if the actress had other plans for him.

If not, he needed to come up with a plan that didn't involve driving all the way home after Steffi dismissed him. He'd check his GPS for an all-hours coffee shop where he could park and wait to be summoned.

They reached the studio gate and Helen bade him to drop her off at the curb so he wouldn't have to execute an awkward U-turn to get out. The second he braked, his phone pinged with a text from an unknown number. Steffi's agent—Suzan, he remembered—requested he come to the house ASAP.

A knot tightened in his gut. Had he done the right thing in taking a long-term assignment? Fares like Helen and other favorite passengers he'd miss, and if they found new drivers what if they decided not to call on him when this job ended?

"Keep at it, sweetie. Make sure there's a part for me," Helen said by way of farewell. Those were her parting words to him after every trip, and he took her hand and squeezed it before she left.

He'd see her in sixty days. Maybe. Assuming this job for Steffi didn't kill him.

His phone chirped again and he realized even the few seconds spent watching Helen disappear behind the studio gates had cost him precious time. When he arrived at the house in the Hills, the garage door opened as he turned into the driveway, with an arm sticking out from the side door waving him through.

Steffi greeted him with a skeptical smile, leaning in the open threshold. She waited for the garage door to rumble closed before speaking. "So you're the Hoke to my Miss Daisy for the next two months, huh?" she asked as he got out.

"That would be me." He gave an awkward wave.

"I almost said Jeeves to my Wooster, but it's not like you'll be the butler. Anyway, the name doesn't seem to suit you."

He rounded the car and waited before her. In her position two steps above him she seemed to relish a sense of authority, yet the cartoon cat design of her flannel pajama pants took away some of the edge she no doubt wanted to project. She wore a yellow tank with it, no bra, high beams alert.

Barry tried to recall if he'd watched a film or show where Steffi had a nude scene. He'd never watched *ViP*. Perhaps now...

"My mom played that role Off-Broadway," she said.

"Must have been a challenge filling Stephen Fry's shoes." That was the only Jeeves portrayal he knew.

"A funnyman. Nice." She huffed and her tits jiggled.

*Focus.* He nodded and trained his gaze to her face. Nobody paid him to play the lech. "Well, I could also be the Kato to your Green Hornet. Actually not."

"Yeah, that scenario's fraught with disaster. Suzan's on the phone, no point in you waiting with the car. She'll be a while." She crooked her neck in invitation.

"Sounds good. I'm—"

He had a hand out to introduce himself, but Steffi spun lazily around, then padded deeper into the house. He followed her to a room off the main living area—a cozier den with a plush couch and matching recliner, both facing a large flat screen airing an old sitcom. From the looks of things—a blanket askew on the cushions, a half-full coffee mug atop an open magazine—Steffi had set up camp here for the morning.

True to his assumption, she slumped onto the couch and stretched out and Barry, to avoid lingering on the border of the room like an idiot, started for the chair.

"There's some coffee in the kitchen if you want," she said when he blocked her view of the TV for a few seconds. "I don't have a housekeeper or cook. Everything here's self-serve."

"Oh. Uh, I'm good, thanks."

Her eyes darted to him, and an eyebrow arched. "You sound surprised."

"That you don't have a staff?" He supposed it was true. Not that he knew Steffi's net worth, but he figured most actors who work in high-end productions had "people".

"I guess I wasn't expecting a casual atmosphere," he said, wanting to groan as he sank into the thick-armed recliner, surprised by how smoothly the leg rest glided upward with the slightest pressure. *Oh, yeah.* He wanted one of these in his coffin.

"I don't have a housekeeper, either," he added. "And I

pick up after myself, so no worries."

Steffi gave a short, humorless laugh. "Well, you're on the payroll, and Suzan walks around here like she owns the damn place, so why not? I don't keep a lot of food stocked, though, so maybe you ought to pack snacks and lunches."

"I'm not a big eater."

Her eyes narrowed and she studied him. "Aspiring actor? Stand-up comic?"

"Screenwriter. Fueled by ramen."

"You haven't done any acting at all? I swear I know you from someplace." She leaned closer as though hoping to trigger her memory, but a raucous joke on the TV turned away her attention and she sank back against the pillows. Barry guessed Suzan, or Donald or some other handler he had yet to meet, had worked through the night to keep Steffi away from the news. That, or Steffi chose not to relive the drama and just chilled.

"You know about this show?" She gestured to the TV.

"It's a bit before my time." He recognized the very young Valerie Bertinelli and some of the other performers. The sitcom as a whole, not so much.

"Me, too, but I love binging on the old stuff. There's so much history, like here," she said, pointing at the TV. "Ever hear of Whitney Blake?"

"No." Would there be quizzes every day? "Is she on this show?"

"She wanted to be. Whitney was an actress. Mostly guest shots on TV in the fifties and sixties. She was the mom on *Hazel* for a while. Her daughter's Meredith Baxter."

"I do know her." *Hottest TV mom since Carol Brady. Yes, sir.* "Rather, *of* her. We've...never met."

*Stop babbling. Where the hell's the agent who needs a ride home?*

Steffi's lip quirked up and she huffed out a laugh. "Well, I think Whitney longed for a better career than Hollywood dealt her. On *Hazel*, she was basically window dressing until they wrote her out altogether, which was understandable

71

because what was the name of the show again?" She shrugged. "She wasn't Hazel so she wasn't the star, and this town's full of pretty blondes looking for work.

"So, the seventies happen and her daughter's getting some action as an actress. She sees an opportunity to pitch a mother-daughter project perfect for them—a sitcom loosely based on her life as a divorcee raising teenagers. She envisioned this as a vehicle for her and Meredith." A sigh, then, "Long story short, the network picked it up and cast other women." She made a spluttering noise probably meant to signify the sound of a career crashing and burning.

"That sucks," he said. At least Meredith had managed to bounce from that setback.

"She did get a co-creator credit for the duration of the series. Compensation, but not much," Steffi said, sipping her coffee. "You say you're a writer. What would you do if somebody optioned your work and did something with it that you didn't approve of?"

"The keyword there is *if*. I'd like to get that far," he said. "Truthfully, seeing my credit on screen would be enough." Also money. And guild membership.

Insurance. Food besides noodles.

The final joke set-up for the episode ended with canned laughter and applause, and the screen split to roll the end credits while the intro for the next sitcom began on the right side. *WKRP*. Barry prayed for the legendary turkey drop episode but Steffi shrank the action even further by calling up the channel guide.

"I read about Whitney's story a few years back, and I think about it often," she said, the remote in her hand pointed at the TV. She zipped through a dozen channels in the space of a few seconds before settling back to the current option. "What discourages me the most is the idea that Hollywood doesn't take female creators seriously, then or now. Here a woman found little to no opportunity and when she tried to make one for herself it didn't pan out the way she wanted."

"I wouldn't say that. If she got the co-creator credit, she

profited from this show, right?"

Steffi glared hard at him. "She *wanted* a lead acting role. It's what *I* want. I had it and blew it."

She huffed and turned back to the TV. Barry wanted to rebut, but instead muttered a weak, "Sorry" before falling silent. He saw no reason for her to shoulder the blame for the demise of her show. Other factors, for certain, had determined its cancelation. The academy wouldn't nominate her for an award if they thought she didn't deserve it.

*Wait…where are we? Right, Hollywood.*

"Anyway, I have to disagree about the lack of female creators. Right now you have big shows started by women. There's Shonda Rhimes, Callie Khouri, Gabby Ran—"

*Whoops. Back up. Should have stopped at two examples.* Steffi's hand, the one holding the remote, drooped along with her head.

"Sorry. Again."

"You got a point, no worries," Steffi said. "Yeah, Gabby made an awesome TV series. I have no doubt the next one she does will be as successful, because she won't rest on this laurel." She nodded toward the kitchen. "Suzan's on the phone with her now. No idea why she called. I thought it might be some kind of PR thing where she can tell the media with a clear conscience that she checked on me."

A call like that would've taken a few seconds. "Is that something she'd do?"

Steffi side-eyed him with a leering smile. "Gabby Randall holds out her arms and woodland creatures gather around to listen to her sing. You wanna go spy for me, hear what they're saying? You can just tell Suzan you're getting a donut."

"Is that part of my job description, and what kind of donuts? Randy's?"

"Winchell's."

"Maple iced?" *Yum.*

She shrugged. "Maybe next time. There's chocolate,

unless I ate them all. I'm a bit fuzzy right now and can't remember."

His stomach cried out to give in. *Go on, be Mata Hari. Snag a free donut.* As he contemplated the assignment, though, Suzan strolled into the den about to speak but paused on seeing him.

"What sayeth the queen?" Steffi asked, eyes on the TV. "Have we been invited to the royal ball?"

Suzan, apparently immune to her client's sarcasm, gestured in a request for privacy. "We have coffee and donuts in the kitchen. Perhaps, you should…uh…"

"Suze, he's not a lapdog. Surely, it won't destroy the fabric of time and space if he listens in."

*Gee, thanks.* It could have come out better, but hearing Steffi talk as if he wasn't there nettled at him.

"Well, it'll come out, anyway, and you'll be driving her there." Suzan sat down next to Steffi, not before ushering her to lift her feet from the couch. "Before I give you the news, darling, I suggest an attitude adjustment. You'll need it when you're back at work."

That straightened Steffi's spine. She muted the set. "We got a reprieve. *ViP*'s been renewed? How would she know that before me?"

"Call had nothing to do with that. Gabby wants you for a multiple-episode arc on season two of *Danse*."

Steffi's gaze panned to him. Her expression no doubt equaled his, a WTF reaction bordering on frowning and hysteria.

"Are you shitting me?" she cried to Suzan. "After all the Twitter bitching, and upstaging her at the awards, she wants to *hire* me?" She looked at Barry. "You watch the show last night? I was on fire, huh?"

"Well, uh…" A scowl from Suzan directed at him helped that decision. *Mouth shut.*

Steffi tucked her knees under her chin and hugged her legs, shaking her head. "What's the deal? Is this some kind of 'keep your enemies closer' tactic?"

"Gabby's not the enemy, Stef. She doesn't think that way of you, either. If it's a PR stunt she hoped to pull off, she'd have brought all the *Wondermancer High* people over for a reunion instead, and to hell with you." Suzan snatched the remote and shut off the set. To Barry, she said, "Sorry if you were watching that, but I need her full attention now."

"I've seen it, no worries." What he wouldn't give for a bag of popcorn to complement this new drama. The apology aside, he no doubt shrank into the far background of their consciousness. Never mind the coffee and Winchell's, he found more nourishment right here.

"Gabby told me she'd written this story arc months ago while planning the next season. She had you in mind for the character all along, and she's really going to bat for you. ExStream wants her to cast another actress, but she wants to go back to them with a firm commitment from you. Given how *Danse* swept the awards last night, ExStream isn't really in a position to refuse her."

"And you gave it to her? A yes from me?"

"Damn straight I did!" Suzan's cheeks pinked. She slammed a fist on the couch arm but the lack of noise against the padded furniture added no intensity to the moment. In fact, the agent looked a bit ridiculous doing it.

"Are you high?"

"I'm earning my paycheck. You know, doing my job? You need the work, too, and you're lucky to be offered this." Suzan rolled forward off the sofa and, with an awkward step, straightened into a standing position. "You're going to play an angel as a counterpart to Dash's Reaper."

Steffi let out a snort. "Talk about typecasting, huh? Not."

Barry thought it wise not to laugh and held his breath for a moment.

"So," Steffi pulled out the word for several seconds, "is there nudity required? Will my character and Reaper have *sex*?" She grinned in a horror clown-mask way, as though relishing the possibility of dry humping her ex-boyfriend while his wife watched from behind the camera. Barry rubbed his forehead, but really sought to shield his smile. What was Gabby Randall thinking, bringing a former romantic rival to her show?

Anyway, an angel. Steffi would keep her clothes on, he assumed, lest Gabby incur the wrath of every church in America. More so, probably.

"We didn't discuss plot details."

"Is Gabby that confident Dash will want to act opposite me? Every chance he gets, he talks about how we almost killed each other when we were dating."

"You're exaggerating. It was one story on a talk show a long time ago, and if Gabby is okay with having you on her set there's no reason why Dash should object. They're married, for criminy, and I'm sure she ran this by him." Suzan brushed off her jacket sleeves. "She hinted at the possibility of making this character recurring, too. With ExStream kissing her ass, she gets to do whatever she wants. I suggest you play nice."

"When have I not given a hundred percent on any show? Give me some credit."

Suzan's silent response indicated one possible example, and when she turned in his direction he knew he wouldn't hear it. "I'm ready to go, if that's okay."

"I'm on y'all's clock. I guess I'll come back here when I'm done?" He looked at Steffi.

"Oh, yes. I'm a busy gal." She flicked on the TV. "People to see, lines to memorize. Costume fittings."

"You officially start today. Gabby's having the contracts messengered." Suzan pointed at Steffi, then nodded at Barry. "I think it's best she lay low for the rest of the day. If you want to go home after you drop me off, that's not a problem. I suggested Steffi contact you if she needs food delivered. We can order online, you'd only pick it up and bring it over."

"Oh, no. I'm not here in my den watching TV, listening to you running my life," Steffi cracked, flipping channels in rapid succession.

"Steffi." Suzan shook her head as though she intended to say more, but instead announced she'd wait for Barry in the garage then strode away. After several awkward seconds spent in silence, Barry moved to follow.

"Yo, Hoke," Steffi called after him and he paused. "I don't know your real name. Unless it *is* Hoke or maybe you prefer I call you that."

He thought a moment before answering. Donald had his information since he'd paid the initial fare, and he assumed the agent knew his name as well. The money going forward would be directly deposited into his PayPal, and they only needed an email for that. If Suzan hadn't revealed him to Steffi, what stopped him from giving a false name? Chances were good he'd only see Steffi. For all they cared, he was one of the little people and they'd forget his name on day sixty-one, anyway.

Steffi still hadn't given the impression of recognizing him from the awards show, and he feared if she found him out she'd find a way to get him or Mags in trouble. One reason he ought to introduce himself as Dirk Skywalker.

*Right.* Did she have the power to see to it he never filled a seat at another Hollywood masturbatory event again? She'd be doing him a favor. *What the hell.* "I'm Barry Spahn. Nice to meet you."

"Yeah." She waved, which he took as a dismissal, but then she asked, "You got satellite radio in your car?"

Yes, and heated seats and a sunroof and Scarlett Johansson in the back seat for whenever he felt amorous. He was a marginally employed screenwriter on a ramen noodle diet. He was lucky his car had tires with tread and gas in the tank, and that RydeAlong deemed it suitable to work.

"No," he said.

"Can it be hooked up? I'll pay the bill."

"Sorry. My car stereo system's not set up for it."

"CDs it is, then."

"Actually," he said, "I have a cassette deck." Not really, but he enjoyed the rise he got out of her.

"What?" She bolted upright and leaned to one side as though trying to see through the walls to his car. "The hell are you driving, the fuckin' Flintstones car?"

"No, it's a 2013—well, like it matters. It'll get you where you're going, and I need to drive your…whatever." He turned to leave.

"I'll see you back here after you've dropped her off," she called after him.

He spun, stepping backward toward the garage. "But she said—"

"She's not your boss, Jeeves."

"Barry." *What happened to Hoke?*

Steffi pointed the remote at him as a warning. "I earned the money they're using to pay you. I'm your boss, and I'll see your skinny ass back here within the hour."

*Yes, Wooster.*

# Chapter Six

Later that evening, Barry drove Steffi to Trader Joe's to stock up on groceries for the week. She wore leggings and an oversized tee, wide-framed Jackie O sunglasses and a scarf around her head. She filled her cart with granola and boxes of frozen appetizers. Despite keeping quiet and paying in cash, the clerk still recognized her and she couldn't get out of the store without signing a few autographs. Most shoppers, though, seemed to allow her space, clucking after her with sympathy as they left.

On Monday, he managed edits and rewrites on fifty pages of an older script before Steffi paged him to escort her to a studio to record her PSAs for the police department, then to a hot yoga studio on Melrose. The class ran ninety minutes, and before Barry worked out in his head what he might accomplish while he waited, Steffi ordered him to Pink's a mile away to stand in line for chili dogs afterward. Barry obeyed and tapped out dialogue on his phone, all the while chuckling at the thought of the actress's choice of after-yoga lunch. She better not attempt the downward-facing dog anytime soon.

On Tuesday, he arrived in the Hills just as Steffi finished signing the *Danse Macabre* contracts messengered by Too True Productions. After speaking at a morning assembly at Hollywood High, she wanted to go to Book Soup and browse their religion section in preparation for the role. "I'm no angel, but if I have to play one on TV, I better learn about them," she said on the drive down. While she shopped, he lingered by the shelves groaning with writer's manuals and published plays, willing some kind of secret energy from them to fuel his creativity. Her presence went unnoticed by the staff, who'd dealt with celebrities of all stripes in the past, as well as some customers.

On Wednesday, following two hours spent visiting every classroom at an elementary school, Steffi craved ice cream. No fast food, brand name franchise slop from a machine, either. She'd watched a Food Network special on mom-and-pop creameries of the US and goaded Barry into driving her all the way to effin' Lompoc, to a shop where an arthritic octogenarian hand-rolled waffle cones made with crushed Oreos and slash or peanut butter. She got a double scoop of cookie dough ripple and chocolate truffle and he opted for the maple bacon sundae, which Steffi kept 'sampling' until he finally had to move to a different table.

On Thursday, Barry stayed in bed as long as possible, filing these treks in his subconscious as the 'normal' excursions. He wanted to forget all the trips in between — the midnight calls to various drive-thrus, the crawl through Bel-Air to pause at the house of Elliot Voller while Steffi debated on pitching a rock at his window, and the six a.m. trip to the beach to visit sleeping seals.

Well, Steffi stared at the fat, loafing buggers and had a good ugly cry over resorting to guest-star shots to pay the bills. He watched Steffi and wondered if she'd kick his shins if he tried to comfort her with a hug.

He checked his phone. Almost eleven in the morning, no inspiration for a new scene in his head and no texts from Steffi to report for duty. He knew she had a meeting with Gabby Randall scheduled for the afternoon, so he'd have to drag his sorry ass out of bed soon. Either she chose to snooze until the last excruciating second or she'd gained a sense of benevolence and decided to give him a break.

*Chirp*, went the phone. Wishful thinking, that. He opened the message screen.

*I want a McMuffin.*

"I want health insurance and a 401k. Whattaya gonna do?" he muttered. As with previous commands, this came out vague. Whenever Steffi ordered things for him to pick up, he had to ask for the store and, more than once, the false name she used for the orders. He didn't understand why she refused to let Southern California's grocers know of her fondness for toffee peanuts and wasabi peas. Here, he suspected he had to get breakfast from a specific McDonald's or else Steffi would turn up her nose at the delivery.

The bubbles in the window percolated.

*You there?*

*What kind of McMuffin? There's more than one.*

*You should know by now.*

He felt her irritation radiate from his phone. He seethed. He hadn't seen her eat a McAnything at all this week. Her last two breakfasts had come from a plastic bag and left cheesy dust on her fingers and armrests.

*Anything else?*

He sighed, thinking he'd buy across the menu board and let her pick the one she wanted.

*I'm good. Use the emergency fund and I'll replenish.*

"Yes, Miss Daisy. Mister Wooster. Whatever." He glanced at the nightstand at the twenty-dollar bill underneath his keys, feeling for a second like a teenager given money for gas by his parents.

He snorted. Like his parents, too, Steffi sure as hell made him work for it.

After ordering at the drive-thru speaker, Barry edged his car forward to make room for the next car and was reaching for his wallet when his phone chirped. He checked the stereo monitor since he'd connected the hands-free option—the only luxury this car featured. His sister Ana in Orlando.

He tapped a button on the steering wheel to accept. "Hello, Hollywood," she said. "Make any millions yet?"

"Still working on it. What's new?"

"Bill took the kids to Disney. I got the day off so I'm doing absolutely nothing and loving it." She laughed. "Well, not quite. I've been fielding texts all day from friends about you."

"What about me? I have no room in my apartment for visitors, if that's the idea."

"You still *have* an apartment? What about this love nest in the Hollywood Hills you're sharing with Steffi Corden?"

*Que?* Time to test out what acting he'd absorbed in his time with Steffi. "I don't know what you're talking about."

"Cut the bull, Bar." Ana snorted. "It's all over the Internet. Pictures, too. The paps have been tracking your girl all over town. She isn't fooling anybody with those head scarves, and since you're not out in disguise you obviously don't care who knows."

In all honestly, why wear one? Barry figured he'd do his job, collect his pay and fade away after a few months. He thought if people snapped photos with clandestine fervor on their phones, they'd focus on the star. This couldn't affect his chances for a show gig later, right?

"Where are you seeing pictures of me with Steffi Corden?"

"Well, I'm not the one hunting them down. Facebook friends are sharing them on my wall. If it's any consolation, it's the same picture of you guys at an ice cream joint...just a thousand websites posting it."

"How nice." The aroma of fried eggs and hash browns assailed his senses and nausea roiled in his gut. The NDA that accompanied his work agreement forbade him to reveal anything, even to family. "I really can't talk about it right now," he began.

"You on the road? Sounds like it."

"I meant in general. When the time comes, you'll know what I can divulge. Uh...Mom and Dad haven't seen any of it, I hope?" Barry knew his parents eschewed much of social media because they preferred to keep their blood pressure at optimal levels. Didn't mean a friend with good intentions hadn't directed them to a gossip site.

"Not that I know of." A pause, then, "What's it worth to you to keep it under wraps?"

He heard the mirth in her voice and nearly missed his turn. "Tickets to the premiere of my first movie."

"Airfare included?"

"Hey, I got student loans still to pay." He wheeled onto the narrow road leading to Steffi's house and paused at the driveway, giving the three-honk signal they'd decided upon to grant him garage access. Heaven forbid some wealthy neighbor spot the help toting Mickey D's into Madame's house.

The door rose to reveal Steffi, trim and chic in pastel blue pedal pushers and a sleeveless white blouse, a designer handbag hanging from the crook of one arm. No sunglasses, no wrap, and Barry saw the shine on her red lipstick from the distance. She intended to show herself today, wherever they were headed now.

They had time before the Too True meeting, which he'd noted in his journal. Steffi slumped into the passenger seat, nearly missing the bag of breakfast he snatched away, and he noticed the polish on her toes and fingers matched the color of her pants.

Her eyelids, too. Actresses made for amazing sights on red carpets and magazine spreads, and all the time Barry saw Steffi 'dressed down' he'd become accustomed to her appearance. This moment...wow. It almost seemed like he was picking up a date.

"You clean up well," he said. He needed something to quash the welling-up mushiness.

Steffi smirked, grabbing the bag off his lap. "Bless you, my son," she said before an exaggerated inhale. "You want the bacon or sausage?"

"Take what you want. I'll eat the other."

"No, you drove all this way." She held up the bacon

muffin sandwich. "You should at least get first choice."

*Really?* "How do you know I don't live in the Hi—oh, who the hell am I kidding? I like the bacon."

"So do I. I shouldn't have sausage burps when I meet with Her Highness, though." She handed him the sausage but Barry waited to take it.

"You sure?" he asked. "You might get some satisfaction with an accidental belch during your *tete-a-tete*." *Damn, I really wanted the bacon*. If only he'd have bought the pancakes as a backup choice, but Steffi might have claimed those as well.

"Given my track record, I'd rather not risk it." Steffi pulled out a hash brown with her free hand and laid it on a napkin. Barry hoped she didn't ask for ketchup. "Suzan's right, anyway. Phone hasn't rung once since the awards, except for Gabby. I need to play nice and claw my way back to mostly hirable."

Made sense. Better to put the best foot, and breath, forward for a comfortable future.

"You're in a good mood today."

"I ought to be. I found out the rest of my community service is suspended." Steffi practically chirped as she talked. "Videos of my school visits went viral, and other schools are asking for copies. Donald used that positive PR to get that to count toward the remainder of my sentence. So I'm basically done."

"Are you serious? How is that possible?" Barry shook his head. This woman was Teflon.

Steffi shrugged. "Hell, if I know. I'm not a lawyer, and it's Hollywood. We work differently."

*Right. So long as you don't kill anybody, whatever.*

Barry unwrapped one corner of his sandwich, took a bite and set it in one of the drink holders before backing out of the driveway. Steffi licked grease from her fingers and sipped from an orange juice carton. "We need to run a few errands before going over to Too True," she said, and summarized the itinerary. First a stop at Donald's law office to pay an invoice, then Rodeo Drive.

He sighed. A trip to the high-end shopping district would mean time spent shuffling his feet while Steffi tried on outfits. Judging from her choice of casual wear this morning, it occurred to him she might want something new to wear while meeting Gabby — a mental boost to show up in a recent design to prove she wasn't ratings poison. He supposed he had the fortitude to sit and hold the purse while she lingered in a wisteria-scented boutique.

"I don't expect Gabby's bringing in lunch, so if you're hungry we can grab a sandwich before then." She waited for the car to stop at a light before drinking more of her juice.

Barry nodded and wolfed down rest of his breakfast before they got the green. He swallowed it down hard without chewing it into mush, and the crisp edges of the English muffin scraped his esophagus. This was why he never ate while driving, since L.A. traffic required his focus on the road. Nonetheless, he let Steffi mess with the radio and chat animatedly about what she hoped for with this acting job. She sounded hopeful for the first time since their meeting…at the awards.

It bothered him that the subject hadn't yet surfaced. Steffi hadn't volunteered to talk about her scandalous behavior that night, save for one moment during the seal-watching trip. *I know the video's gone viral, but I'll unplug altogether if it means never seeing it.* Two seconds later, she was taking selfies with the giant beached beings in the background and uploading them to Instagram.

If she did remember him, what he could do? Grit his teeth and face the consequences, he guessed. At best, he could leave her employ and return to his old life — alone in an efficiency with his screenplays and no human contact.

He turned onto Wilshire, driving closer to Donald's office. Steffi talked about soup now, in particular the matzo ball special from the deli just off Rodeo, and wouldn't that work better for lunch after all this heavy food?

*Yeah, I could go for a bowl.* One for himself.

He glanced to his right and noticed how Steffi leaned in as she talked, her elbow on the center console, her lips bright red and full enough to kiss.

He wouldn't dare, though, again. Sausage breath.

*Right.*

\* \* \* \*

"How is Mr. Spahn working out for you?"

Mr. Spahn, now waiting in the car while she dashed off a check on Donald's assistant's desk, ought to praise the gods for such a chill job. He'd mentioned something about aspiring to write, but in the past week she'd seen nothing on him to indicate as such. If he brought a laptop or notebook to use in between car trips, he must have tucked it under the driver's seat. She couldn't recall him typing on his phone, either. Well, nothing to end up in a screenplay.

When he went home…she guessed he worked. Doubtful. Between the field trips to Lompoc and the beach and the midnight snack runs, he had to have felt run ragged. Not that she relished keeping him out at all hours…she just hated staying home without something to occupy her mind. She'd worked with regularity since coming to Hollywood. Young, cute and blonde had gotten her a number of commercials before a soap producer had created a role for her. Alone she could handle so long as a script kept her company.

She realized she waited so long to answer Donald's question. She ripped the check away from its perforated pad and surrendered it. "He's nice," she said. "He's done everything I've asked. He's not acted untowardly." Man, that sounded weird coming out of her mouth. "And I think he'll do for the rest of my probation."

"I'm glad to hear it." He glanced down while his assistant created a receipt. "You'll be glad to know your money is well spent. Ms. Appleton will serve no further time and was only charged a small fine."

Marleen Appleton. Steffi stretched the name in her brain for a few seconds and nodded. The woman had a name, and perhaps other people named Appleton in a state out east thought of her and waited by their computers for e-mail or a text message saying she was okay. Parents, siblings, loved ones Marleen had refused to blood sacrifice in exchange for fame and fortune. What studio did that? The idea of something so sinister almost brought up her egg sandwich.

"Does she need help paying it?" Steffi dipped into her purse. "I got some cash—"

Donald's large, dark hand crossed her line of vision, hovering just over the zipper. "Ms. Appleton asked us to relay her thanks to you, nothing more," he said, then frowned. "It's no guarantee she'll change careers."

"It wasn't a stipulation of my getting her a lawyer. Thanks." She slipped the receipt in her bag and bade goodbye without inquiring of her legal troubles. She'd left Barry in the car long enough, and she needed him in good temperament for their next stop.

Before he'd come to the house, she made a reservation under his name for a parking spot in a nearby garage and paid with cash she handed him, all the while hiding her face behind her bag until they pulled forward. Barry glanced at her with amusement but said nothing until he reached their assigned space and killed the engine.

"Why all the cloak and dagger just now? You weren't bothered when people recognized you at the grocery store, it seemed like."

"I'm a celebrity. I'm not allowed my unexplainable quirks?"

Barry's right eyebrow raised, almost to his hairline. She laughed—he came off rather cute with his WTF expression, like a beleaguered sitcom boyfriend. Man, forget having that kind of complication in her life right now.

"Grocery stores are different. Everybody has to eat, and it's not bad for your image if you venture out to buy your own spaghetti and eggs. Gives the impression we're like, regular people, right? I know Suzan would prefer I order food and have you pick it up until the worst of this publicity blows over, but the other day wasn't so bad."

He nodded, scratching the side of his nose for a second. "True. No middle fingers pointing in your direction."

"Rodeo Drive is...well, you know." If Barry did, he refused to volunteer. "It's upscale, la-di-da. I strut around here like Miss Hollywood and people might think I don't give a fuck about my image."

"Image." He scanned around the car and out of the window for a moment, as though waiting for a better explanation to happen. "You're a public figure, presumably with money to burn, enjoying a day in a high-end shopping district. What subversive message do you believe you're broadcasting? Tabloid junkies expect *that* of you, at least."

Yes, it sounded ridiculous when he dissected the situation, and she wanted so much to make sense. She imagined babbling through a meeting with Gabby and coming out like a total bimbo. Maybe she wasn't ready to go back to work. They ought to pull out, forget the parking fee and go home to classic TV and leftover, stale donuts.

A loud clunk and a zipping noise startled her. Barry had released his seatbelt but remained in place. "You're about to have an important meeting and want to shop for an appropriate outfit. Who cares about that? It's nobody's business but yours where you buy clothes," he said and hit the unlock button. "So where we headed?"

"We're not here for me, Barry."

His eyebrow went up again. *Wait a minute...*

"What's wrong with what I've got on?" She glanced down at her clothes—all crisp and pressed and clean. That she'd managed to finish her McDonald's without spotting the linen pants she considered a miracle.

Barry shrugged. "Dunno. It's a bit casual for a meeting designed to reignite your career, I thought."

"Yeah? How many Hollywood meetings have you

attended? What's the dress code?" she snapped. Barry didn't flinch, but she felt like crud nonetheless. She had no right to call him out like that, especially since if this coming encounter with Gabby went south she might in the same boat as he — scraping along on crappy jobs until she recovered. And she had no license right now, so it wasn't like she could make extra coin as a rideshare —

*Wait a minute.*

"I remember you now."

*Oh, crap. Welp, fun while it lasted.*

He'd have Donald direct deposit what money he earned, then go home and turn his RydeAlong profile back to active. No harm, no foul, his life back to working-poor normal. Like hell she wanted a constant reminder of the most humiliating night of her existence driving her around L.A.

Funny, she seemed calm as she spoke.

"You drove me home from the police station. All of us," she said, her gaze panning to the empty backseat then to the dashboard. "I mean, I don't remember your *face*, but the last few days I've sat in this car and wondered where I'd seen it before."

"That's it?" he asked. "All week I drove you around SoCal and you didn't connect me to the guy who brought you home in the first place?"

"Well," she sounded sheepish, "Suzan said the next morning she and Donald hired a guy. I wasn't a hundred percent sure you were the driver from *that* night. Could have been somebody else."

"Fair enough. No more details come to mind?" Like, a kiss in front of the free world?

She frowned. "No. We pretty much drove from there to the house."

*Okay, false alarm. Perhaps.* A total recall was still possible. Barry thought of the extra money he stood to make and tried to deflect. "Well, a car's a car's a car. If you're concerned, I signed an NDA with your attorney—"

"Yeah, I know." Steffi sputtered out a noise and waved him off. "I just wish I remembered everything about that night. I can't bring myself to watch the videos or search the news. I already have nightmares about poverty, why compound it?"

"Right." A knot tightened in his chest. The car's interior shrank around them. "We're paying for this spot by the hour, right?" He checked the rearview mirror—shoppers laden with hoity-toity-looking bags clipped along in high heels to their respective cars. Each appeared involved in her own world, but they'd soon attract stares if they didn't move. "Where are we headed, and why are we here if you're not clothes shopping?"

"I am, though," she said, "for you."

"Oh." So she was embarrassed by *his* image then? "You're not buying me a livery, are you…?"

"No, Jeeves." She rolled her eyes. "I figured, since we may end up at a big event in the next month or so as a result of this *Danse Macabre* job, you should have a nice outfit or two, just in case. Blend in better. Consider it a gift—it won't come out of what you're making."

"Ah." Well, he'd be a fool to refuse nice clothes, seeing as his wardrobe consisted of T-shirts and jeans and little else. He hadn't bought anything new since leaving Florida save for what he called his 'meeting the agent' suit.

"I appreciate it, but really… If you want to get me clothes, let's go to a department store. Rodeo's a bit much, you think?"

Steffi gave him a stern glare—not furious, more motherly than anything, and it sort of unnerved him. "Hey, you want a life in Hollywood, you have to dress the part, no matter what you do. Besides, there's another store around here we need to see to get some boxes."

"Putting things in storage?"

"Packing things to move, namely your stuff into my house."

# Chapter Seven

*Wha – ?*

The word echoed in his head, all through the brief fitting for a blazer and two pairs of pants, through an interlude in which Steffi signed autographs and posed for group selfies, through a so-called light lunch of six-inch-high pastrami sandwiches. He nodded and muttered answers when prompted, and gave the illusion he paid attention to his charge and the world around them. Moving in. She wanted him in her house, twenty-four-seven.

She intended for him to leave his sanctuary. Granted, as a home it stank — only an idiot would insist on staying with his silverfish buddies in an efficiency not worth the triple-digit rent. His mind wandered to Steffi's hillside deck and that breathtaking view of the city, the firepit surrounded by cushy lounge furniture perfect for early evening napping in cool breezes. Steffi didn't have to give him a spare room, he'd just live out of a backpack and hang there.

He understood why Steffi was driving this. Proximity made things easier. No thirty-minute lags in a midnight In-N-Out craving, plus if Steffi had concerns about his being impaired while driving, she only had to corner him at her house and smell his breath.

Then he remembered his conversation with Ana, and the gossip connecting them as a couple. "Aren't you worried about people will say?" he asked. "You've admitted you pay attention to how people perceive you...so you want lips flapping about how you're moving a man into your home?"

Steffi was chewing a bite of her lumberjack sandwich, and

it took a few seconds for her to swallow and breathe again. She sipped from her can of cream soda. "You're not a bad looking guy. At best, the press will say, 'Go me'."

"I'm flattered. Not just saying it. I like my privacy, though. I worry if I'm this close, I'll be driving you places around the clock."

"You won't. Even I have to sleep."

"Suzan will not agree, yes?" he challenged. The agent appeared straight-laced and all about protecting her client's image. Living with a man, the horror.

"You're an employee, like a butler. Jeeves Hoke Smithers. If anybody asks, that's the story." She shrugged and, after sizing up what was left of their lunch, grabbed for the napkins. "We'll make this dinner tonight. We gotta motor if we're going the make it to Too True on time."

* * * *

For once, they made good time in town, meeting every green light and finding few cars impeding their route. Barry pulled into the fenced lot of Gabby's production company with minutes to spare, and as Steffi checked in with the young as a zygote receptionist at the front desk he searched for a comfortable spot in the waiting area. It resembled the set of a seventies daytime talk show — it only lacked a bubble machine and a gilded curtain backdrop.

"Ms. Randall is waiting for you, if you'll follow me," he heard the girl say. He glanced up from his inspection of the Brady Bunch's sofa to notice Steffi disappearing down a hallway.

"Guess I'll be here," he muttered.

Seeing no magazines of interest to occupy him, he settled in for the wait with his phone opened to the writing app he used to touch up his scripts. He saved his work on a cloud server and could access it from any machine he used. He preferred his laptop for ease of use, and while the app allowed him to magnify text, he only worked on his phone if given no other option. The scene in this particular screenplay, a tense conversation between a mother and her grown daughter about the possibility of moving the family's patriarch into a hospice, gave him frights. He cursed through every correction and line rewrite, unable to hear the dialogue flow in his head.

He contemplated chucking the scene altogether, but leaving it out risked a gap in the story no other action filled so well. Maybe bring in a third character to liven up the argument? His right heel bounced against the shag carpet, the silence surrounding him unnerving, but he focused on the tiny blinking cursor on his screen until a shadow fell over his peripheral vision.

"Hey, seat warmer. Small world, ain't it?"

Hot gravel and botanical flowers. *Holy cow, she remembers me?*

Randi Marsh's cloying perfume assailed his nose and he turned away for a moment, thinking he might sneeze. The woman standing before him had transformed from the wild-child vixen who'd hijacked him at the television awards. She wore no makeup and had her color-streaked hair in a ponytail, and sported a faded Ramones T-shirt with skintight jeans. A thin cardboard package was tucked under one arm.

He liked this look. All-natural and kick-ass, like she was off to give the PTA hell.

He began to stand to greet her, but Randi cackled and waved him back. "Hey, we're all casual here. No need to curtsey." Randi flopped down on the opposite end of the couch. "So, you meeting Gabby or you here about the job?"

"Uh..." *Job, there's a job? Like, a writing job?* Writing episodes for the hottest show in the country? A line on his resume that would take him anywhere in this town.

His heart lodged in his throat and he willed himself to breathe steadily and slow, reminding himself to face reality and assume Randi probably meant there was an opening for a production assistant. AKA, the guy making the Starbucks runs.

"I'm actually on the clock." He nodded toward where Steffi had disappeared. "I drove Steffi Corden here."

"Oh, yeah. I heard about the deal her lawyer cut with the HPD. Watch whiteness work, eh?" She crossed her legs and the cuff of her jeans slid upward, revealing a tattoo on her ankle — a skull impaled on a diagonal railroad spike. A logo from an old Randi Raucous album? It looked familiar.

"I suppose." No point in arguing. Best to play conservatively in the event he could benefit from Randi's presence. "I assume you're with Gabby after she's done."

"Eventually. Later in the day, maybe. I just stopped by to add this new shiny to my office." She held up the package. Barry noticed one undone flap and a flash of dark color. Without further prompting on its contents, Randi opened the thin box to reveal her directing award nomination certificate in a distressed wood frame.

"The academy gave us these things done up like plaques, like the kind the Shriners have put up in seafood restaurants where they meet. Too stuffy." She frowned. "I had mine reframed to go with the décor. Wanna see?"

"Really?" A big-time TV director was inviting him to see her office, in the hottest production office in town. And he tasted sausage and plastic cheese every time he spoke.

"I'll behave," she promised with a chuckle. "It's not gonna be Christine Grey bringing some unsuspecting virgin in for *dick-tation*." Snort. She slapped his leg and leaped upward. "C'mon! Nobody ever comes to see me at work."

He said nothing, and couldn't felt his legs as he lifted himself from the couch and followed her down the same hallway that had claimed Steffi. His insides flipped and fluttered, all giddy like a girl about to meet her favorite boy band. After years of trying to break into the business, simple as this, he was entering the nerve center of Too True Productions.

All he had to do now was figure out how to come back again, on his own.

* * * *

"This is the preliminary storyline. Scripts are still in draft, and I hope to have working copies over to the cast as soon as possible. Of course, you know how it goes with episodic television. I can guarantee there will be changes."

Once in Gabby's spacious office, windows looking out to the main road, Steffi took a moment to appraise her surroundings. Gabby hadn't wasted any time in marking the territory as belonging to an industry success. Framed magazine covers — Gabby smiling down from various trades and women's monthlies — lined one wall, and a shelf behind the desk held an array of trophies. She saw crystal torches and retro-TV-shaped awards, accolades given by Viewer's Choice associations. Plus, the biggest one of all, the trophy and the envelope Steffi had held that night, stood among them.

On Gabby's desk, a silver frame displayed a photo of Gabby and Dash at a modest chapel, flanked by an actress friend and a Johnny Cash impersonator. Vegas wedding, how tacky yet quaint. Steffi hadn't been able to get Dash to cross that state line the entire time they'd dated.

"Do you have any questions for me?"

The bubble popped and Steffi jerked her head toward Gabby, who pushed a sheaf of papers fastened by metal prongs toward her. She took the thin bible for *Danse Macabre*'s second season and shook her head, idly flipping the pages. "Not at the moment," she said. "I think my only concern is if, in the rewrites, my lines start to disappear."

"I don't anticipate that. Rafaela plays a crucial part in this new story arc. I want to be sure you're a hundred percent comfortable with the concept." Gabby paused and cleared her throat. "And what the character does."

"Is this about the sex? I've done love scenes on camera before." Hell, her character on the soap had been the town tramp, hopping into bed with most of Poplar Valley's men.

"What about nudity? Not just bare asses, Steffi.

Everything."

*Uh.* The egg muffin sandwich popped and fizzled inside her. *How many calories was that?*

"And sex scenes with other women. And men. Plural." Gabby leaned closer. "I know *ViP* wasn't that kind of show…"

Damn straight. On a show like hers, only the male politicians got to roll around in the sack. The lady Vice President cut ribbons at museums. Still, the idea of being set up between two hard-ons like a pig on a spit intrigued her. "Is this *Danse Macabre* or *Deep Throat* we're doing here?" She dropped the packet.

The remark made Gabby laugh out loud. One point in her favor toward keeping this job. She was no prude, but it felt weird talking about near-porn with the wife of her ex.

"Steffi," Gabby said after she settled with a deep breath, "you haven't seen the first season? Not even the first episode?"

*Seriously? We're going there?* Why would Gabby think she'd make time watch a TV show starring a guy with whom she had an explosive relationship that had ended with acrimony? Steffi guessed people assumed she'd check it out with morbid curiosity, as a means of masochism, but in truth she watched so little television. She had yet to view *ViP* as a finished product.

"I suppose it's essential to understanding this role." She picked up the secured papers again. At least Gabby didn't snatch it away and order her to leave.

"Steffi, I know you've had a rough patch—"

*Understatement of the year.*

"So have I once. Same with Dash. Phones weren't exactly ringing for us the second *Wondermancer High* went off. This show didn't happen overnight, either. About half a dozen networks turned Lina and me down before ExStream offered us a contract," Gabby said, her eyes taking on a misty appearance. "At one point I was close to filming the damn show in my house with my phone and uploading segments to YouTube, and hoping it made a viable revenue stream."

"Oh, lord." That sounded worse than dinner theater. "I haven't set the world on fire myself, but to this point I was steadily working. More than others can say."

Gabby gestured to the show bible. "You still have work. It's five guaranteed episodes in the story arc now. How about it?"

* * * *

"A spinoff?" Barry said.

Randi leaned back in her chair and propped her Converse-shod feet on her desk. "Assuming viewer feedback is positive, it's a done deal. Gabby could tell ExStream she wants to do a miniseries on making cheese and they'd greenlight it. They are in love with her."

Barry let the news sink in, all the while panning his gaze around Randi's private space. Her office resembled a miniature rock-and-roll museum exhibit for all the signed photos of musician friends, the framed gold and platinum records, and the guitars propped in one corner. "Gotta have one in my hand. It helps me think," she'd told him during the brief tour. Now the announcement that Gabby wanted Randi to take the lead on *Fallen Angel*, the *Danse Macabre* spinoff hopefully starring Steffi, burned in his mind.

She'd need writers. Randi had talent, sure, but she'd have her hands full directing and producing. Gabby didn't write every show on her own, either. Randi needed team players.

He needed twenty-four units of credited work to join the WGA. If he remembered the requirements, he'd earn four units per story written...so six episodes of *Fallen Angel* and he'd be in the guild. Insurance, benefits. Maybe easier to land an agent and get his film scripts optioned...

"Anyway, that's between you, me and the Gibson over there." Randi pointed at the cherry-red guitar closest to the exit. She righted herself to standing and started for the door.

"Far as I know, Gabby doesn't plan to break the news to Steffi today because she'd rather concentrate on her show. So, I'd appreciate your lips staying zipped—"

"Let me do it. Please."

*Damn.* A novice freshman begging the football coach to put him in the last play couldn't sound more desperate. Randi paused in place and regarded him with bemusement.

He stood. "I'm a writer. I have two completed feature-length screenplays but I'm not wedded to film. I want to tell stories, doesn't matter where or how. To work on a project for ExStream is a dream come true, an amazing opportunity." He caught the skepticism in her eyes. "Uh, if there's a chance of it."

"It is a dream," Randi agreed. "*Danse Macabre* was a dream, so is Gabby Randall."

He smiled. She hadn't said no or fuck off. Yet.

"But—"

Barry steeled his body, waiting for the rejection and the ejection.

"*Danse* is a known quantity now. *Fallen Angel* isn't." Her expression darkened. "Neither are you."

"With all due respect, was ExStream that confident *Danse* would be a hit?" he challenged. "What if it had flopped?"

"I guess. Still, it doesn't mean automatic success for *Angel*. Some spinoffs tank." Randi resumed her path to the door. "And I do need to get my ass in gear with a production schedule."

She paused, hand on the jamb, and smiled at him.

"Tell you what." She picked her wallet from her back pocket and handed him a business card. "I have no idea how vetting writers works. Gabby's going to help, and at least two *Danse* writers are moving over. You know, I like you, too. You put up with my crap at the awards and I think that's worth compensating.

"E-mail me a few sample scenes so I can get a feel for you, and I'll send you an NDA. Sign and return it, and I'll give you a copy of the show bible and a, ah, test run." She winked. "Think you can handle working for a tough old broad like me?"

This should have been Barry's cue to respond he'd work with the devil for this shot, and while Randi might have laughed he imagined his devout mother sensing the blasphemy all the way from Florida and later giving him grief. Instead, he shook Randi's hand and agreed to the challenge before exchanging goodbyes.

He was back in the lobby when Steffi emerged seconds later, folder in hand. "You hungry?" she asked. "I could kill an animal-style burger at In-N-Out."

"Sounds good. My treat." He had a gift card with some credit left on it.

Steffi pursed her lips with mock impressiveness. "Big spender. Something interesting must have happened while I was gone."

Barry followed her out the door. No jinxing his chance. Lips sealed. "Not really, no."

\* \* \* \*

During one of her first television auditions, for a thirty-second chewing gum ad, a casting director had ordered Steffi into a lineup with half a dozen other hopefuls. Like many calls, this one had been specific — late teens-early twenties blonde, good skin and teeth, come to this office wearing shorts and a tank top. She'd almost balked at the requisite attire, but her mother had warned her how Hollywood wove sexual threads into every aspect of media. Somebody must have convinced the good people at Mint-A-Fresh that consumers trusted bouncing tits to recommend the proper brand of gum to them.

She'd stood there like a pageant hopeful while a balding man had leaned in with his pockmarked nose and inspected their every curve and dip, each exhale a pained whistle. He had dismissed three girls after a few seconds, announcing to the room they were too fat.

To this day, she recalled their tears and stifled boo-hooing. They'd looked fine to her — at worst the girls had been maybe a dress size larger than she. She had gotten the boot next because her earlobes were all wrong. She didn't understand that at all. It wasn't like they were Dumbo-sized and guaranteed to distract viewers from a packet of gum.

After telling this story to Barry over cheeseburgers and fries smothered with grilled onions and special sauce, she added, "When I was approached to do *ViP*, I had it in my contract that nobody could give me grief about my weight. Back in my soap days, some actresses were contractually bound to maintain a certain dress size. I hear it still goes on. Can you believe that shit?" She grabbed two fries dripping with orange sauce and folded them into her mouth, each chew a small victory. No fasting for roles or mandated weigh-ins for her, not anymore.

"Surely, the industry's changing," Barry said. "I see plus-sized actors on TV often, and not as the butt of a joke or as the dumpy, sexless sidekick."

She had to concede to his point. Still… "I think Hollywood has a ways to go to reach full body positivity. Until I see a superhero with stomach rolls as she flies away, I'll remain skeptical." She sipped from her soda cup. "You get any writing done during your break?"

He shifted in his seat, looking around. "Not much, but after this talk I feel the need to go back and rewrite a few scenes."

"Oh?"

"My first script is kind of based on my mother growing up in Miami, not long after Castro took power," he said. "Her parents managed to get out beforehand, but they still had family there. Have." He shrugged and stared down at his meal as though contemplating the next bite. "She talks about aunts and uncles she's never met, not sure if they're even alive. It inspired me to write a story about growing up, imagining a place where you have family a little over a hundred miles from you and being unable to communicate with them."

A veil of sadness seemed to drape over their table. Steffi thought of her mother, also in another country yet accessible, and how she couldn't muster the interest to punch in a text message to her.

"Well, that will change, right? Relations with Cuba are opening up, Castro's dead, and I'm sure we'll be able to travel there freely again. You think your mom would go back?"

"She's never been. She was born in Florida," he said. "Of course, there have been ways to get around travel restrictions, but she always said no. I guess maybe the picture of Cuba in her mind is the one she prefers, and with her parents gone, she might feel it isn't right. I don't know."

"You could ask her," Steffi pressed. When Barry glared at her from the lip of his shake cup, though, she figured it best not to continue this thread. Family and work, no doubt sensitive subjects, and she looked around for another point of interest. She'd signed a few autographs on coming into the restaurant, and right now diners left them alone. Just the occasional phone pointed in her direction, probably for Snapchat snark. *Calories, Steff. Tsk, tsk.* Insert piggy-face emoji.

*Like it's anybody's damn business what I choose to eat.*

"What was that?"

She jerked back to Barry. Shit, she'd started muttering to herself. How much longer until she started collecting cats? "Nothing, sorry." She lifted her burger to finish it off when something caught in her peripheral vision. Big hair and webbed stockings, a flash of color from shiny fabric. She turned to see a familiar figure standing in line to order. In the space of two seconds, her brain waffled on whether or not it would be a good idea to acknowledge the person, but Steffi's mouth overrode all common sense and called out, "Hey, Marleen."

A few people in line turned in her direction, but only Marleen's eyes widened in presumed surprise. Steffi excused herself from Barry's company to greet her. "How are you?"

"A bit shocked. I didn't think you'd remember my name, what with you…" Marleen pressed her clutch purse close to her chest and she moved her head side to side, as though checking for eavesdroppers. Everybody else in line had their heads lowered to phones. The two women could have stripped bare to no reaction.

"I'm an actress. It's a job. Trust me, I'm not the diva snob the media makes me out to be," Steffi said. Well, at least she'd vowed recently to act nice. Now to wait for the world to notice.

"I was thinking there was a chance they might have brought you in for reprogramming after the awards. Or cloned you. They do that, you know." Marleen edged closer in a conspiratorial whisper. "You see these girl singers with vacant stares. It's all animatronic technology used by the government."

Steffi bit her lip and nodded. No point in arguing. She'd crossed paths with a few pop stars in the past, and many had wooden personalities. "I assure you. I'm the real deal."

Marleen's stance relaxed. "Thank you for helping me out with, you know. I can't repay you — "

"I'm not asking you to. Are you working tonight?"

Marleen stiffened again, prepared to defend herself, but Steffi added, "Just be careful, all right? Condoms, condoms, condoms. And save your money. I got this." They shuffled to the front of the line and Steffi stood by while Marleen recited her to-go order, then paid with a phone app. "Take care," she said and shook the woman's hand.

Marleen mouthed a thank-you, and Steffi saw no vacancy in her eyes. When she turned back to her table, she almost bumped into Barry, holding an empty soda cup.

He had the same misty expression and smile.

"I was…about to get a refill," he said, shaking the ice. "You want anything else?"

"I'm good, thanks. I think we're about done here." As

they cleaned up, a couple approached for a selfie and she obliged, all the while Barry supervised with the same expression of…what? Awe, or perhaps admiration? How much, if any, of her gesture to Marleen had he witnessed to change his attitude?

She tried not to ponder it on the drive home, but Barry spoke to her in a soft voice and with frequency. During the first week of his employ they'd exchanged few words and endured awkward silences. She'd attributed some of that to adjustment — getting to know each other, and a bit of each of them hoping the other harbored no murderous intent. Now that she felt comfortable around him she expected they'd warm up, but the way he glanced at her as he drove…

It was like they were coming home from a date.

A message pinged on his phone as the garage door closed on them. "That suit you had me measured for is ready," he said. "That was quick."

"The perks of fame," Steffi said, dropping her house keys in the bowl on the kitchen table where she kept a fanned stack of store loyalty cards and loose stamps. Hearing this news reminded her they'd forgotten to swing by Barry's place to pick up his essentials. She still thought it necessary for him to stay over until the state lifted her license suspension, but that moony moment at the burger joint nettled at her. *Give it another night,* she decided. He'd probably forgotten.

"You need me for anything at the moment?" He waited by the open side door, his feet rocking on the threshold. "You got an idea of your schedule tomorrow?"

Yep. Either that, or he was pretending she'd never offered him a room. "No meetings, unless Suzan books one at the last minute. I'll text you."

She thought to wave him goodnight and move deeper into her house. Get into her pajamas and lie in bed with her eyes closed, waiting in vain for sleep. He feet moved in the opposite direction, toward him.

Into arms that parted wide to accept her, and wrap around to clasp her back as Barry pressed close.

"What are you doing?" she asked.

He shrugged. "You did something good for somebody tonight. You deserve some credit for that."

*A hug is credit?* Steffi thought of the last time she stood this close to a man without cameras filming it, and she blanked.

"Are you uncomfortable?" he asked. "Should I stop?"

Steffi met his eyes.

"No."

# Chapter Eight

*What if she remembers?*

Barry kept a loose hold on Steffi, his hands just skimming the upper curve of her backside as though searching for a place to rest without breaching a forbidden boundary. Not that any part of Steffi turned him off — she had a cute bottom. He'd noticed its hypnotic sway the evening she stormed off to hijack the limousine. He never expected one day he'd come so close to touching it.

He slid his lips over hers, parting as hers did, mating with quiet need. He watched her closed eyelids flutter and it looked as if she'd fallen into a trance, kissing him as a young girl might practice with a pillow. All this time, he should be enjoying an intimate moment with a gorgeous TV star, yet his mind persisted...they'd kissed before under different circumstances. What if the feeling became familiar to her and all the humiliation rushed back?

Worse yet, what if she *didn't* recall? Granted, their onscreen smooch happened as a poor attempt to save her some face, but it'd also mean he hadn't made a memorable first impression.

Why did he overthink everything? *See, this is why you don't date much. Aside from the holing yourself up at home and writing all the time. Which hasn't gotten you anywhere, either.*

*Who in the what, now? Right. Kissing a starlet.*

He pressed firmer on her back and she inched closer. Her thigh brushed the front of his jeans and a faint tingle bloomed in an area long dormant. Nice to know the equipment still worked without self-stimulation. They kissed more and let time slip from them as they swayed in place and synched their breathing, no other focus but their mouths, tongues and waking desires.

A memory surfaced. Something about Steffi wanting him to move in with her. Not for this reason, of course, but he pondered the wisdom of staying here if it turned out neither of them were able to resist a moment of lust.

Fingers brushed his bottom, then up to hook into his back belt loops. An upward yank pulled his jeans tight against his crotch, which hardly helped stave off his growing erection. Then a weight began to tug at his knees.

She'd lifted one foot to meet the small of his back. Good lord, she was trying to scale him like Everest. It left Barry to cup her ass as she wrapped her legs around his waist. He stepped forward, kissing her through the awkward trek across the kitchen and into the hallway leading to her bedroom. He hip-checked the breakfast table and the blunt edge of the sink counter, then rattled a few pictures hanging in the hall when they knocked to one side.

He broke away, gasping for air but more concerned with seeing where they were going. "So, like I was saying, if you really don't need me for anything more…"

"Uh-huh." Steffi kept one arm draped around his neck and carded her free hand through his hair. "I kinda want to stay in tonight. Nowhere I have to go."

"That's good. Traffic's a bitch around this time. I'd know." Not a complete lie. He'd driven various shifts with RydeAlong to get a feel for the best times to drive and slash or write. This hour — whatever it was at the moment — was really bad for getting in a car and rolling out of the Hills to a place where no kissing happened.

She stuck out an arm, cutting the air through an open doorway. Left turn signal, into her bedroom. He'd never seen it before — he stuck to the common areas where he'd seen Suzan pace, often sitting in the main living room and yearning to try out that back patio. This room…he liked it, despite the dimness. Steffi kept the décor understated and comfortable with blue sheets and curtains, a vanity loaded with makeup bottles and tubes, and nearly bare walls. He hadn't stepped into a diva's perfumed boudoir, but then again, he hadn't come to sightsee.

* * * *

Steffi heard a muffled thump and realized Barry's knees had hit the side of the bed. She remained wrapped around his torso, pecking and nibbling at his lips like an inexperienced teenager. Damn, but she'd let too much time pass since her last kiss, last fuck, last grope. She'd had a fling with a co-star from her soap, which was okay for her, but she'd gone into that expecting a quick end to the affair. Every time a bit player showed interest in her, she suspected a two-pronged motivation—free pussy and a career boost.

Only Dash had showed no intent to use her to revive his status in the industry. She supposed she owed him credit for that much, but he was the last thing she wanted to think about right now.

She wanted the hands cradling her in strong arms to slide around and cup her breasts, stroke over sensitive skin and seek out other places ignored far too long. His growing bulge tapped the underside of her thigh with every sway and step and she yearned for something harder and thicker inside her.

How had they gotten to this point? He had one foot out the door and she closed the distance and bypassed the kindling, going straight to inferno.

She craved a connection—anything to sate the hunger veiling her skin. Gabby wrote a TV show drenched in sex, and no doubt had inspiration pounded into her regularly. And Marleen...sex was her *vitae*. Everybody got some but her.

Time to change that. Barry was good-looking, and appeared clean, eager to learn about the industry. Why not help with casting couch practice?

"What was that?" he asked with a chuckle after tilting

back his head. He released their kiss when she'd snorted into it, the sex audition thought causing her to laugh. The pause should have doused their momentum but Steffi shook her head and relaxed in his grip to let her weight fall toward the bed.

"Nothing," she said. "I'm great. I'm feeling this is like a scene I don't mind doing over and over."

He released her and she fell back with a yelp, bouncing on her rump. Barry kicked off his shoes and pulled away his shirt. Hello, muscles and abs and pecs and bare skin.

"Back at the restaurant, when I saw you buying dinner for that woman," he said as he worked on his pants, "I had feels for that moment, if it makes sense. You reached out to somebody. We all need to do that more."

"I bought a sex worker a hamburger. Not exactly a Mother Teresa moment."

"It's more than what some people have done. Everybody's judgy. You treated her like a person."

"Thanks." *Charity is sexy, noted.* When Barry lost the pants and briefs all thoughts of their earlier dinner and the outside world flew right from her head. No tan lines. He sported an even shade of light brown skin and a cute butt, more so when he bent to retrieve a condom from his wallet.

With her clothes shed and tossed to the floor, they savored skin on skin action, touching and kissing so much she lost track of time. Barry settled between her legs and explored every dip and curve. Fingers kneaded her breasts and slipped low to massage her clit. All the while his tongue mated with hers, leaving her unable to see his shadowed face.

So long as he kept up the hot finger action, though, she had no problem with looking into the dark, or a blurred image. Barry worked her body with expert ease, though, enough to drive her thoughts away from details and toward the orgasm pooling like a lava pocket in her belly. A few kisses, timed to his slipping one finger inside her while his thumb took over control, sent her over the edge. She grasped his shoulders and let her head fall back as she cried out.

She reached for him, to reciprocate, but while her body still sizzled he rolled away to sheathe himself. *Oh my...* Well, no matter, it could wait for another time. Given the choice of where to feel that impressive wood bobbing closer as he brought himself to lay over her again.

He kissed her once more, deep and demanding, and guided himself into her. The sensation, one she'd missed forever, curled her toes and she locked her legs around his to keep it real.

"You are so beautiful," he said on a sigh, and brushed her lips against his neck. It sounded odd to her ears. Her partners never talked during sex. Not that she wanted to reflect on that. She whispered a thanks and returned the compliment by grabbing his solid, muscled bottom, squeezing with his every thrust and letting herself go in the moment.

He climaxed with a shuddering breath in her ear and a mumbled "Damn," before collapsing to her side. Panting deep to slow his heartbeat, she assumed, he pulled her in tight and peppered her neck and throat with kisses. "If you say I have to live here for the next month I don't think I'll want my own room," he said.

Steffi laughed, but said nothing. Any reply from her might come out misinterpreted. He'd need space of his own for privacy, and she knew she snored — she'd woken herself up more than once. The novelty of an all-night bed partner was certain to wear off after a few go-rounds, and Steffi wasn't sure she wanted that.

Sex with Barry again? Definitely something to consider.

\* \* \* \*

She woke with the sharp urge to pee and forced herself to stand. A peripheral glance at the bed revealed Barry, as she had predicted, hadn't stayed. Her post-coital honking had no doubt irritated him. Whether he'd taken refuge elsewhere in the house or had left to go home, she had no idea. She didn't feel like prowling. She had to get some sleep and look refreshed for whatever Suzan planned for her in the morning.

She'd received scripts for *Danse Macabre* but expected rewrites, so she wasn't worried about memorizing lines just yet. At best, she intended to use some time to get her head around this character Gabby had dreamed up for her. Angel cop, yin to the Reaper's yang. No real talk of nudity, but Steffi figured that wasn't in the cards for her. A naked, rutting angel, even on a streaming network, posed all sorts of controversy.

Steffi thought about her contract for *ViP*, and the nudity clause Suzan had them put in which gave Steffi right of refusal. If she shot a nude scene and didn't like the end result, the show was obliged to cut and destroy it. Of course, a show about the Vice President lent few opportunities to show the world her boobs, anyway.

She finished her business, washed her hands and padded back to bed. The brief glow of her phone alerted her to a message – a news item about her had gone live…at two in the morning. Fame never sleeps.

*Steffi Corden on for 'Danse', Playing Local Samaritan.*

The headline covered two separate topics, her new job and the dinner she'd bought Marleen. She swiped through to find a picture of her chatting with the prostitute just before their turn at the In-N-Out register. The accompanying article speculated on her motive for being nice, and some sources had misidentified Marleen as a homeless person.

"Duh," she muttered. Only in L.A. was an act of charity viewed as PR. The more she thought about it, though, it was possible Marleen had no real home to speak of. She might be holed up in a low-budget hotel like the one that had inspired a recent horror anthology series. Steffi shuddered to think about sleeping on a urine-soaked mattress, fifty locks on the door to keep out bad elements.

She moved her thumb to scroll the rest of the article, which turned out for the most part to be a rehash of her award show nosedive. An embedded video teased a photo of her walking toward Gabby to interrupt the other woman's speech. The frozen expression of confusion, mixed with fear, on Gabby's face made Steffi cringe. She held no memory of the moment, swear to Heaven, yet it seemed every person in the world had seen it. Judging from the look of the crowd watching her approach, it must have been epic.

She was tempted to press play on the video. With the event in the past, it had no chance of hurting her now. She proved it by getting a role on *Danse Macabre*. Once people saw how well she acted, more offers were certain to come in. Do more good, and this video became a forgotten footnote in her career. Nobody talked about What's-His-Face getting caught with that hooker anymore.

This wasn't *that* bad, assuming she hadn't let loose a string of racial slurs.

*Damn it. Now, I have to do it.*

The video filled her phone screen, the sound vibrant through the speaker. Gabby's voice called out loudly over the din of applause, then softer as the clapping faded. Faces with smiling expressions floated in the background — none of them emitted the high-pitched squeal that signaled the camera to pan with a jerk to Steffi, storming mid-stage.

"Holy crap," she muttered. Raccoon eyes. When had she cried that night? Somewhere between the last Jack and Ginger and the *Danse Macabre* theme song blaring as Gabby's crew gathered for their circle jerk.

She poised a thumb to pause the action when movement in the crowd of onstage onlookers caught her attention. A familiar figure, cut nice in a tuxedo and cringing with discomfort, burrowed through bodies to get her attention. "Mother fuck," slipped from her lips as Barry dipped his head closer to the mic in an attempt to diffuse the situation.

Why hadn't he said anything before about his being there?

With Hollywood being a smaller town than outsiders perceived, Steffi figured she'd run into Barry once or twice in the past. The only plausible reason for his presence on that stage was he had gone to escort somebody from *Danse Macabre*. Paid or free, she didn't want to know.

Why he was kissing her now in this video…a question she wanted answered.

Steffi rolled out of the bed, beelining for the door.

\* \* \* \*

The Randi Marsh-vampire theory formed in his mind held some water. He wasn't the only one stirring in wee-hours LA.

After slipping out of Steffi's bed, plagued by insomnia, Barry settled in the TV room with his laptop. He stretched on the couch and sent Randi an e-mail with a sample of his most recent spec script, an episode of a popular medical drama he'd chiseled on for dialogue practice. Minutes later, the reply came with two PDF attachments: a non-disclosure agreement from Too True Productions and Randi's first draft of the *Fallen Angel* show bible.

*How would you write up Rafaela* — Rafaela being Steffi's celestial heroine — *confronting a drug lord?* came the accompanying message. No further hints, no setting, no context. Randi had given him a challenge, and either he needed to ability to see into her vision for the Rafaela character or the showrunner hadn't quite figured it out herself. It worried him. What if he turned in a scene Randi really liked, but didn't get a spot on her writing staff? Once he turned in this sample, she'd have *his* vision of Rafaela and what stopped her from applying it to the show?

Barry had mixed with other writer hopefuls when he first came to California, all of whom had shared nightmares of breaking into the business. He used to meet them at a coffee shop near the Hollywood Farmers Market once a week to commiserate and share industry gossip…until the rejection stories had gotten too depressing and he'd made excuses to no longer join them.

As he wrote now, one particular story from a lady screenwriter filled his memory. She had doctored a film script for an employed friend, rewriting more than half of it. Details were fuzzy, but somebody had managed to spot a loophole in the agreement she'd signed and she'd never gotten paid or credited for her work. The friend had never gotten his name on the screen and more offers as a result.

Randi Marsh may come off as all rah-rah and support the underdog, but Barry's fingers on the keyboard slowed as he considered the alternative. The rocker turned TV director possessed survival skills, and beyond the awards show and a brief meeting in her office he barely knew her. What guarantee was there that she wouldn't appropriate his writing without compensation?

*Money, feh.* He could *make* money for the time being, enough to keep his rent paid, but he had to have an in, into the business. He sallied forth with his script, but the worry it was all for nothing lingered in the back of his mind.

The light illuminating the next room took care of the front. Steffi appeared in the entryway, a mussed-up beauty. She'd thrown on a tank top and sweat shorts and now stood there with one arm propped against the jamb of the wide entrance, watching him with a bleary expression.

"Why don't you turn on a lamp or something?" she asked. "That screen glare can't be good for your eyes."

"It's okay. I have one of those apps that adjusts brightness levels to the surrounding light. Plus I take a few breaks, averting my eyes, blinking long..." Well, they may have just engaged in the most awkward post-sex greeting since discussing the weather. Steffi's current facial expression, coupled with her stiffened body leaning like it was propping up the wall, told of her obvious nervousness. She had the look of a woman wanting to say something, but needing prompting.

"I'm sorry if I woke you," he said. "I couldn't sleep, I'm usually a night person, and I figured why not burn off the energy with work?"

"You didn't. I had stuff keeping me awake, too." She stepped deeper into the room and took the recliner, reaching for the remote. "Just thinking about this new job. As long as I've worked in TV you'd think there wouldn't be any more jitters, but I still worry." She pointed the remote and fired. "You don't mind, do you? I'll keep it on mute."

He shrugged. Her house, her TV, her money keeping him in ramen and gas. He wasn't going to tell her what not to do. Besides, if she insisted on hovering near he wouldn't get much more written, television noise or no. He preferred solitude when it came to finding his groove. It was why he passed on having roommates, and gave up on writing at coffee shops while people texted and snapped and blathered all around him.

"What are you working on?" Steffi leaned forward in her chair, but from the position at which Barry sat on the sofa she had no way of seeing the words on the screen. On instinct, he saved the script and closed the document before looking up at her.

"Touching up that screenplay I was telling you about," he lied. "I was thinking about what you said about talking with my mom, getting her perspective for the main character, so I kept a chat window open while I typed up notes."

"Night owl runs in the family, huh? It's gotta be midnight in Florida."

Barry nodded. "She likes her late-night shows." His gaze panned to the TV and the infomercial for an elaborate vegetable peeler. *Mmm, zucchini fries.* "I've revised this thing about ten times already. What's one more draft?"

"Back when I worked on the soap, we'd get rewrites in the middle of shooting." Steffi tucked her long legs under her seat, and he caught a flash of bare thigh when she shifted. Weird to believe only a few hours ago he'd touched her there, had thrust inside her and come harder than with any other woman. Here they chatted like old friends.

She stroked her knee, and the mere gesture—while innocent—turned him on. He squirmed a bit and moved his laptop to hide his growing bulge.

"Sounds like a pain in the ass," Barry said.

Steffi laughed. "Well, contracts would come up and the actors would leave, so lines for one character would either go to somebody else, or the scenes would get cut altogether," she explained. "Occasionally, too, a producer spotted a continuity error to fix, or else fans would bombard the show with emails." She rolled her eyes. "Like, you can't have Sally get a phone call from Tim six months after he fell into a woodchipper."

"The hell kind of soap opera kills off a character that way?" To his knowledge, even *Danse Macabre* hadn't played that card.

"Soaps are made of crazy sauce, are you kidding?" Steffi flipped channels. "We had people walled off alive in basements… Oh, this one villain bitch kidnapped her ex-husband's fiancée and amputated body parts a bit at a time."

Barry's stomach churned. He remembered watching 'stories' as a child with his paternal grandmother. Raciest behavior he'd ever witnessed had been a drink in the face.

"Started with fingers and toes. Turned them into chum for the sharks at the marine science compound where her son worked." Steffi chatted on about this scenario, the profession of which sounded implausible and outrageous to Barry's ear. In that moment, he realized the reason why he'd had trouble getting his writing noticed. It wasn't batshit crazy enough.

"Then finally Vanessa—she was the villain—had enough of Corinne's screeching so she dragged her down to the shark tank with the intention of chopping off her head and tossing it," Steffi continued. "Of course, her ex, Derek, showed up in time, there was a fight, and Vanessa goes head first and becomes shark bait."

"Why didn't she just…never mind." For a cold, calculating soap nemesis, Vanessa lacked smarts. She could have lopped off Corinne's head in a safer place and toted it in a bowling bag to the aquarium. Less dramatic that way, though. "That must have been an interesting reunion for Corinne and Derek, assuming she survived."

"Yeah. Vanessa only got as far as the left lower leg. Then there was this whole story arc about Corinne getting artificial limbs and falling in love with the doctor and leaving Derek at the altar for him."

*Holy crap.* "Unbelievable."

"I know, right?" Steffi shrugged. "The girl playing her won the Best Actress award that year."

"I meant I'm going to have to cut all those 'loose fingers in the shark tank' scenes out of my script. People will think I plagiarized."

He said it so deadpan it got Steffi to cease her channel surfing. She gawped at him for a second before bursting out with unladylike laughter. "Good one," she said after recovering with a loud snort.

Barry tapped the top of his computer. "I should be so creative."

A noise broke the silence, something like an old bicycle bell. Steffi had her phone tucked in her shorts and she checked it to announce Suzan had booked her to appear on a morning show in a few hours. "We need to be there before six for makeup. Said she's texting you the address."

Sure enough, his phone cried out for attention. "Your agent certainly earns her keep working around the clock," he murmured.

"She's half-vampire on her father's side, insomniac on her mother's."

Barry waited for the accompanying blood-sucker comment, because agents, but Steffi instead stood and stretched. "No sense going back to bed," she said on a yawn. "You want some coffee? There's a deli that delivers twenty-four-seven. I'll call up for breakfast."

"Sure anything without—"

"Apricot jam," she finished, "because you're allergic. Side of syrup to dunk your pork products and coffee black with two stevia packets. Got it. I got clean towels and bar soap in the spare bathroom if you want a shower."

Steffi didn't turn back as she left the room. Barry watched her disappear, amazed by how much she remembered of his food preferences. He hadn't thought her to notice anything about him.

Opening his laptop, he called up the *Fallen Angel* script and stared at the blinking cursor by the last line of action. Steffi ought to know this about him as well, so why did he want it kept secret?

* * * *

Their order completed and paid for, Steffi closed the deli's ordering app and called up the video of Barry kissing her, replaying it muted. She'd had him right there but said nothing. Anytime during their conversation, she could have leaned over all casual-like and asked, "Hey, what was all that with you kissing my drunk ass on live television?" Instead she had talked about bad soap plots.

Maybe it had embarrassed him and he wanted just to let it go away. No blame to give there. What would come of her calling it to attention? In a way, too, she guessed bringing up the video forced her to relive that humiliation. She wanted to move past it.

Still, she would have liked to know tonight wasn't the first time they smooched.

*The last time, though?* Part of her hoped not.

# Chapter Nine

It had taken a few years, but Barry finally got to stand on an actual soundstage. Granted, it was the set of *Funshine L.A.*, which only aired statewide and in parts of Arizona and Nevada, but they legit had cameras and sets and people in headsets and clipboards scurrying to and fro. After escorting Steffi to the studio, one such person directed him to a modest green room where he nabbed a few miniature donuts and watched the live program.

Steffi, bright and chirpy despite lack of sleep, turned on the starlet charm and joked with the hosts about her last live TV performance. She took their ribbing in stride and even played off her behavior that night, all the while steering the conversation when she could back to her new role. Barry admired her restraint. Nobody appeared interested in her upcoming acting gig. They wanted the dirt.

"She's doing good. Those jackasses need to stop interrupting her, though."

Barry nearly choked on a bite of donut. Suzan appeared out of nowhere to stand right behind his shoulder. He turned to see her head bent, thumbs tapping on her phone screen.

"Hey, I didn't know you'd be here. I could have swung by and picked you up."

"It's okay. I'm too far away from here or Steffi's to make the trip," she said.

"Oh, but..." Not true. He'd dropped her off at her at her place in WeHo before. What was...

And he turned farther to see Donald Quinton, dressed smartly and seated in a chair along the wall, steeping a tea bag in a foam cup. Their eyes locked for a few seconds and they acknowledged each other with smiles and nods.

Quinton, if he remembered from overhearing talk between actress and agent, lived all the way out in Brentwood. Too far from the Hills to drive, like Suzan needed a ride from there.

*Two and two together, just like Suzan and the lawyer, apparently. Gotcha.*

"Oh, now, this can't be right," Suzan muttered, bringing his attention back.

"What?"

The agent ignored him, and glanced up when Steffi entered the green room. Barry checked the flat-screen on the wall and saw the show had gone to commercial.

"Hey, you." Steffi waved to Donald before addressing Suzan. "I think it went well."

"I'm glad you're in a good mood, because I just got word from Too True."

*Oh, shit.* Suzan's tone and frown lines seemed to dampen the mood in the room. If Gabby had decided to hire another actress after they all got up at the ass crack of dawn to help promote her show…

"Gabby's changed the production schedule for their next season. They're moving up filming the eps with your story arc."

Good news. "So, I start work earlier, that's fine," Steffi said. "When?"

"Tomorrow."

"What!"

Suzan pocketed her phone. It must have been a signal for Donald, because he stood and approached. "Randi Marsh was offered a slot on the bill of some eighties nostalgia rock tour. She wants to get her work out of the way before she goes." She gestured toward the door. "Revised scripts are coming to the house. You best get to learning lines."

"Jeez. I'm okay with short notice, but surely Gabby can get a new director for those shows instead of rescheduling,"

Steffi grumbled, and followed Suzan and Donald out the door.

"Gabby has her reasons," Suzan said. Of course. With Randi in charge of *Fallen Angel*, she had to work with Steffi to determine if they were a good fit.

Barry knew it, and it was apparent he was the only one in the room. Randi had sworn him to secrecy when he wanted to shout to the world that he might be one step closer to an actual Hollywood writing job.

Damn it. The schedule change meant he needed to get his sample to Randi, like, now. If Randi embarked on a tour who knew how long she'd be gone, and if she'd remember him when she got back?

"Let's meet up for lunch after your first episode wraps. Send me your shooting schedule when you get it and we'll work something out." Linking her arm with Donald's, Suzan waved a quiet goodbye before leaving. Barry bounced on the balls of his feet, eager to get back to his laptop. Probably wouldn't hurt, either, to slip a peek at those scripts if Steffi gave her the okay. Damn, though, he needed to get to his place and pick up some more clothes. What he wore now, from yesterday, was good for the time being, but—

"We have to go get your suit." Steffi checked her phone. "Is your apartment on the way to or from Rodeo?"

Her words spiked through his thoughts, and he reached for his keys and followed her to the exit. "Easier to stop by my place first," he said, working out the map in his head. Steffi wasn't listening for all the attention given her by the morning show's crew.

Once inside his car and on the road, she spoke again.

"You know what? I think I'm going to call Gabby and see if she'll let me out of this."

* * * *

"What!? Why would you do that?"
Whoa. When had Barry started channeling her agent?

They paused at a stoplight and he focused all his attention on her, looking as though she'd announced her intentions to swim to Hawaii. It baffled her. Like her career choices affected him. He'd get paid to drive her regardless of whether or not she worked in the next month. Better to make quick trips to the coffee shop than slog through L.A. traffic to sites on location, assuming Gabby had planned such scenes for her.

"It's no big deal," she said. "I've turned down shows before. Saying no hasn't killed my career. I just did a morning show. Something else is bound to come my way."

"Don't you think it's a bad idea to decide this right after you told *Funshine L.A.* you signed on? A recurring role on the hottest TV show in the country right now, and you have no reason—"

She held up a finger. "Hey. It's not on you to decide when I'm ready to go back to work. I'd be happy to do *Danse Macabre* on the schedule I originally agreed to. I was going to use the time before shooting to center myself."

*Don't you roll your eyes, you wannabe chauffeur.*

"Tomorrow is too soon for me. It's been a rough few weeks for me, and I don't feel I've recovered."

Yeah, she'd brought much of the misery and bad press on herself, but to prep at short notice for an early morning call? She lowered the passenger side sun visor and checked herself in the mirror. With the makeup still intact from the morning interview she looked fine, but underneath there existed a very tired woman. How was she supposed to turn up fresh for a new role in under twenty-four hours?

"You really need that long of a break between jobs?" Barry asked. "People go to work every day of their adult lives, many without a vacation. Life is hard."

"Yeah, and maybe that's why our country is fucked up at times," Steffi countered. "This mentality that you have to work all damn day and get stuff done at the speed at light. Some countries in Europe, they have mandatory vacations. It's why they aren't as high-strung as Americans."

"Well, what about Suzan?" They neared Rodeo Drive and he checked the streets for a spot near their destination. "She'll lose her shit if you try to back out of the show."

"Her job is to find me more work and more money, *when* I'm ready for it. Even after my pratfall at the awards I'm still her best client. She won't walk."

"Chances are she won't allow you to let this opportunity go. Gabby isn't going to like recasting your part at the last minute."

Steffi turned his way, her lip quirking up at one side. "Do you drive a lot of out of work actresses around to auditions? I mean, when you're not at home writing the Great Cuban-American Movie?"

She watched for his reaction. She hadn't intended to come off as triggery and rude, and Barry clenched the steering wheel for a moment before shrugging. "Most people I drive are in the business, but not always actors. The ones who are manage to find steady gigs and don't bitch about 'me time'."

"Anybody famous? Besides me."

"You'd recognize faces." He frowned. "You suggesting I should pass on a tip to one of my regulars? There's an old lady I like who's more suited to playing the Reaper's grandmother."

"Eh, forget it." Steffi's head lolled side to side on the back rest and she stared out the passenger window. "One day, I'll be playing grandmothers. I should live so long."

Happy talk. Like she anticipated supporting roles as a tart-tongued elder while younger actresses took on meatier parts. Post-fifty seemed like a good age to pursue stage, which was kinder to older women like her mother. Maybe she ought to order a copy of *Auntie Mame* to memorize just in case.

The trek to the men's boutique for the suit and the detour home by way of his apartment happened in tense silence, interrupted by monosyllabic sentences and grunts. Barry seemed almost afraid to open his mouth, as though a suggestion threatened to catch fire in the air between them and spread into an emotional inferno. Or, perhaps he was embarrassed to have her in his modest living quarters. She'd refused to wait in the car like a dog.

It looked more like a hotel room, where he lived, and he had no reason to feel shame. Her first Hollywood apartment had resembled a closet by comparison, and she'd had roommates to boot.

Barry brought only one suitcase with him and a stack of books, all scriptwriting and style guides. Back at her house, she set him up in the guest room her mother used when in town. Barry said nothing about the floral-print sheets and lavender room freshener Regina favored.

He tested the bed. "This is nice," he said. "Much more comfortable than what I have."

"You can tell from just one sit?"

"Compared to that concrete slab on a springboard that came with the place, this is a cloud spun by angels."

"Your ass must be thanking you." She wanted to sound smart, but disappointment panged her heart. He'd said nothing about the possibility of sharing her bed again, and in a way, it hurt. Never mind that he might be going for proper gentleman and considering her feelings here. Being with him the other night had reminded her of the cravings and pleasures she missed.

She clasped her hands together and thought for an out. "I suppose I have homework," she said, thinking of the scripts they'd found earlier at her door, left via express delivery. "I'll order in Thai, so enjoy your evening off."

"Steffi."

She turned from the doorway. "Yeah?"

He patted a spot next to her. "I'm a better writer than I am a tap-dancer. Maybe let's use some words to talk about last night, so the remainder of my stay isn't all awkward and weird facial expressions?"

*Right.* She heaved a sigh and returned. She didn't flinch when Barry's thigh brushed against hers.

"What we did…you liked it, I hope?"

"Oh, of course." She had trouble meeting his eyes. How weird. She'd never been filled with nerves talking sex with anybody before. Not with Dash or prior lovers. She'd had flings with co-stars in the past with whom she shared less in common yet she still managed a flirtatious air whenever she saw them.

What was Barry, but a regular guy? Very handsome, skilled in the sack, but not what she'd consider relationship material. He'd be sleeping on his rock bed in a matter of weeks, anyway, maybe that was it. She told herself she didn't want to get too close.

For his sake. For his feelings.

Yeah.

"I liked it, too, and not just because you're a TV star," he said, and added when those words made her turn. "I'm not a star fucker. I promise you, there won't be stories sold to the gossip sites."

"Some of them are reporting you might be more than an… employee." In truth, no media site had yet revealed Barry's purpose for being here. Suzan wouldn't have bothered with a press release—Steffi knew her agent would want to keep the deal with the Hollywood Police untold. Fat chance, but a nice thought.

He shrugged. "I know. My phone's been lit up by all my family, wanting the details. I've said *nada* to them."

"Thanks."

He nodded, then took a deep breath himself. "Like I said, I don't profit from intimacy, so if ever you're feeling lonely…"

He let the unspoken invitation hang. It wasn't a romantic declaration designed to turn her wet, but she nonetheless found his sudden modesty endearing. She leaned over to kiss his cheek. "If you're not careful, I may just take you up on an offer," she whispered, her voice husky. "Pad Thai all right by you?"

"And spring rolls with peanut sauce?"

"Ooh, baby." In a fit of laughter, she strolled from the room.

* * * *

Somewhere between chicken pad Thai and the next morning's coffee, Steffi found the confidence to go forward with her *Danse Macabre* story arc. The necessity of a paycheck, in light of presumed dwindling funds, no doubt played a factor, too.

The next two weeks saw the two of them lapse into a comfortable routine of early morning calls and late drive-thru runs, interrupted a few times — often after her filming intense scenes — with a sweaty tumble in the sheets. Knowing Steffi needed her rest for the next morning's shoot, Barry slipped away with reluctance to the guest room after their lovemaking, but he considered the boost to his creativity good compensation. When Steffi worked, he was granted permission to hang in the trailer reserved for guest actors. He used the time to write, and two weeks in Steffi had her scenes for three episodes of *Danse* in the can and he two spec scripts for *Fallen Angel*.

With Randi directing the arc, he'd run into her a few times. Thank the entertainment gods, she'd loved his writing and commissioned story concepts based on a rough series outline.

Still no firm offer of a contract, though. He'd have felt more comfortable with something signed and legal, but after surrounding himself in Too True's atmosphere he got caught up in the show and the crew's enthusiasm. Now, he just had to get Randi to make a real commitment to him.

"Helpful note, short of snuff and bestiality, anything goes with this series, just like *Danse*," she'd advised one day. "I want writers who not only think outside the box, but cut holes in it and fuck it raw."

Rather than deal with paper cuts on sensitive spots, Barry soldiered ahead with a few script ideas. Being close to Steffi, he hoped, gave him an advantage over other writers Randi might have courted, and as Steffi headed into week three of this job he fantasized about seeing his name on *Fallen Angel*'s opening credits.

All the while nursing a thread of guilt.

He'd told Steffi he wasn't a star fucker, yet realized the possibility of connecting his work for Randi to them, assuming word got out that he'd become her driver with bennies. Then he'd remind himself that he'd talked to Randi about writing for her *before* he had slept with Steffi, and that getting a job with *Fallen Angel* hadn't come guaranteed. *His* talent had to seal the deal, not Steffi's celebrity.

So, here he sat, in the guest trailer, waiting for the day's shooting to wrap. He put the finishing action on a scene, saved it then opened a browser to peruse his social feeds. His sisters communicated mainly through them, sending pictures of nephews and nieces and appraising him of family exploits. They'd learned not to prod about Steffi and he deflected any hints they wanted to know more about his famous passenger.

Tonight, he got lucky. He sat at a round table in the guest trailer, typing away while sipping from a can of soda, when a voice sounded from distance beyond the propped-open door.

"Y'all decent in there?" called out Dash before poking his in for a look. Barry had seen a number of actors up-close during his time in California, driven a few via RydeAlong, and he'd come to the point where the starstruck giddiness had worn off. Not with everybody, though. Like many people his age, he'd grown up on *Wondermancer High* and dreamed of meeting at least one of the teen wizards. Seeing the original Freddie "Grody" Grodin coming through the narrow threshold to greet him nearly inspired Barry to squeal his appreciation. He managed to hold it together while the two shook hands.

"You're waiting on Steffi, right?" Dash reached into the mini-fridge for a grape soda and took a seat.

"Yeah. I'm her...driver." He held up his visitor pass to confirm the permission given to him to be here. "Guessing it won't be much longer?" Shooting tended to wrap close to midnight, and the clock on Barry's laptop read eleven-ten.

Dash nodded. "In a bit. I'm done for the night, which is great since we're all off tomorrow." Barry didn't know that, and figured Steffi might say something later, and Dash volunteered no further information. "So, what's it like, working for Steffi? She treating you all right?"

"Of course." Barry searched for something in Dash's expression to determine if the actor showed concern for him, or else fished for information on Steffi's private life. Barry knew — hell, the whole world, too — of Dash's past with her. Maybe the guy wanted to show friendly support.

"Steffi's been great. She was excited about being on your show. I hope it leads to better things for her." *And me.* Why would he not want that for himself?

"You never know." Dash shrugged and pulled long from his can. "Anyway, I just came in to see if Padge was still here." He referred to Cory Padgett, who was also appearing in Steffi's arc. "I didn't mean to interrupt your writing. Randi said you were scripting episodes for her, huh?"

Barry's heart surged at that. Why say anything to others if she had no intentions of hiring him? "Actually, yes. Taking a break now, so you're good."

Dash smiled. "Randi's the best. If I had to work with one director the rest of my life, she's it. She's a team player, one of the few people who lets writers hang on set." His eyes then narrowed. "You haven't seen her in action yet, have you?"

Barry shook his head, and before he knew it Dash was out of his chair and gesturing for him to follow.

"We'll be fine. They're almost done with the last scene for the day. You ought to get at least a glimpse of how she runs things," Dash said and was out the door, giving Barry only a few seconds to close his computer and trail behind.

His throat died, entering the hot set. In the three weeks he spent here, he'd only gotten as far as the trailers, and with Dash so close nobody appeared ready to pull him away. As they approached he saw bright lights and equipment and bodies moving in shadows. Steffi stood in a space done up to look like an office. She wore a snug business suit that accentuated her figure, and when she paced in front of the desk occupied by another actor Barry couldn't help but check out her curvy bottom.

Randi stood near the camera, expressionless and focused on the action. Dash gestured for Barry to stand with him, out of the way, and watch in silence. No problem there. Steffi in action proved enthralling to watch. Her stunt at the awards show aside, he'd seen her in clips from *ViP*, but this live performance confirmed her acting ability.

He knew the gist of this episode. Steffi portrayed a government agent charged with apprehending Reaper, but the outlaw's paranormal abilities allowed him to escape the police with every suspicion. This argument between Steffi's character, Rafaela, and the town sheriff flowed so naturally. Being familiar with Steffi's temper, Barry became caught up in her acting style and thought for a moment she wanted to wallop the guy with his feet propped on the desk.

"Aaaand, cut!" shouted Randi after Steffi slammed the office door behind her. A buzzer sounded and lights dimmed, and many shoulders sagged with relief. Steffi rounded the false wall holding the door and let a production assistant help with her hair.

"Let's keep that one. Great job, everybody." Randi clapped her hands and turned in a circle to regard the cast and crew. She caught sight of Barry and winked. "I got band rehearsal in twenty minutes, so I'll see y'all bright and early Thursday."

"This late?" cried the sheriff actor, who strolled past on his way to the craft table.

"Gotta practice if I'm gonna tour." Randi grinned and dashed away.

The man turned toward Dash. "I bet those rumors about

her being a vampire are true. When does she sleep?"

"Far as I remember, she only played a vampire on TV," Dash said in defense.

Barry enjoyed the banter, but his attention drifted to the activity before him. The crew was breaking down the set, jotting notes on clipboards, packing up leftover food in the craft area. Part of him wanted to imprint the memories forever in case he never got this close to a TV show again, plus he wanted to get his bearings and be ready to write scenes set within the industry.

*Write what you know…*he wanted to learn it all.

"Hey, what brought you out of your hidey-hole?" Steffi came up from behind with a coffee cup and tapped Barry's shoulder. On seeing Dash close by, her demeanor iced up a bit. Barry thought it weird — they'd been working together for a while, but maybe they hadn't defrosted to the point where they could be friendly.

"I thought your driver might want to see where the magic happens," Dash offered with a nod of his head. "You were very good, by the way."

"Thanks. I was getting a bit winded with those last few lines. I hope it shows well on film." Steffi put the back of her hand to her mouth to stifle a yawn.

"If Randi says print, it's a done deal. I trust her on that." Dash glanced away for a second and gave his goodbyes, then moved to catch up with Gabby, but skidded to a halt after a few feet.

"Steffi, you coming tomorrow?"

"Oh, I haven't decided," she said, casting her gaze downward.

"Call Gabby if yes. She'll text directions."

The studio seemed to empty of people after that. He followed Steffi out to the car — she remained in her outfit. "I'll come back Thursday wearing it so we can complete the sequence." She fanned out her fingers, showing off two rings and a silver watch. "This has to come back, too, for continuity."

"I'll remind you if you need it," Barry offered.

"Thanks."

Closer to home, they paused at a light and Barry turned to her. "Where do you need to go tomorrow?" He liked to have addresses or at least a general area in his GPS beforehand.

Steffi frowned for a second then shook her head. "Nowhere that I know of. Suzan hasn't booked anything, but I might go to the gym and I'll let you know when I want to go."

"What about whatever it was Dash invited you to?"

"That." She snorted. "Some mucky-muck at ExStream is having a party. I'd rather shove an icepick in my eye."

The very same icepick that stabbed at his senses, he guessed. What he wouldn't give for an invitation to an industry soiree. "You think that's a good idea, skipping out? I mean, it's the mucky-mucks who keep y'all employed."

"Eh, I'm fried. Those mucky-mucks got us working all hours."

Well, that might have been Gabby's doing. She co-owned the company making *Danse Macabre*. ExStream just cut the checks and put the finished product online. Besides, Steffi and the rest of the cast and crew had tomorrow off, Barry guessed, to be fresh for this party.

Crossing at the green, Barry spied an empty space along the curb and tucked in.

Steffi grasped the handle above her passenger window and gawped at him. "What are you doing?"

He killed the engine. "I'm about to talk some sense into you."

\* \* \* \*

"The way you're acting, you ought to consider switching your career aspirations to management," Steffi told him. He seemed to think he knew what was best for her. He had no experience. Steffi's recent award show *faux pas* aside, Suzan hadn't nagged her like this, especially over a dime-a-dozen industry yawner.

"Steffi, I like you. I mean, obviously." He gave a nervous, short laugh. "You are damn lucky to be where you are now, and I'd hate to see your second chance with ExStream go away because you're feeling meh about one lousy social event."

"It's a party. It's not midterms."

"It's opportunity, and somebody's ego," Barry countered. "If you're a no-show tomorrow your mucky-muck friend will nurse the burn for a long time." He eased back in his seat and his eyelids grew heavy. "I want to tell you a story."

"All ears." She checked the sidewalk, gauging her exact location. Still a fair hike back to the Hills, but close to her favorite burger chain. He was buying the milkshakes after this to compensate for her suffering. "I suppose I should picture Sicily, 1920?"

"More like La Jolla, two years ago. I went there for a conference and became acquainted with some fellow writers. We attended the same panels and hung out at meals, had a good time. On the last night there was a late cocktail hour where all the conferees could mingle with people in the industry. Lots of book agents and editors, but nobody involved in advancing a screenwriter's career, so I wasn't all that enthused.

"These guys I was with convinced me to tag along, and I did...for about fifteen minutes," he continued. "I was like you about this party, just a bunch of mucky-mucks standing around talking and drinking. I faked a headache to excuse myself and went back to my hotel room to watch TV and dink on a script." He stared out the windshield, his expression darkening further in the shadows crossing his face. "Come to find out one of my convention pals stuck around and ended up chatting with an agent who asked to see his work. Next thing you know, he's got a three-book deal with one of the Big Five pubs." He slammed his fist on the steering wheel. "To this day I keep thinking if I'd stayed something like that could have happened to me."

"I've heard this story before, Barry. Not yours exactly, but different variations, one from my own mother." Everybody had a similar tale of regret. If only I'd dined in the restaurant instead of getting takeout, Spielberg would have noticed me, and so forth. "What if you had stayed longer? There's no guarantee you'd have an agent now as a result. Anyway, you said there weren't any screenwriting agents there, so why you mad, bro?"

He snickered at the change in her voice, a blatant attempt at humor. "That *friend* with the book deal? I read in *Variety* about a major bidding war between studios for the film rights to the first one. He's closer to Hollywood than I am."

"No kidding. Is there a part for me?" She batted her eyelashes. No laugh that time. "Okay, are you still in touch with him? Sweet talk him into letting you adapt the book."

Barry cranked the engine and checked his mirrors for a slot to move forward. "Come on. You know the odds of that happening."

"People beat odds. Ask the Cubs."

He raised an eyebrow at her. "Actually, they were statistically the favorites—"

"No. No mansplaining." She pointed toward the burger joint. "Milkshakes. It's been a long day."

"Fine, milkshakes. Afterward, we'll talk more about missed opportunities."

Steffi groaned. *No letting this go, huh?* "If I agree to put in an appearance at this party, will you lay off?" she asked, her tone sweet.

"I'll lay off, lay down..." He let the innuendo hang between them for a second, drawing a response from her with a grin.

"You know what?" She pointed away from the drive-thru. "Skip the milkshakes. I'm in the mood for something sweeter."

# Chapter Ten

"What is so damn funny?"

Barry's frame shook as he asked. It was clear he wanted to keep from laughing along with Steffi. Indeed, it seemed silly for her to break out in giggles while kneeling naked in her spacious shower, but once Barry joined her and she went to work on his impressive, hard cock the humorous thought refused to leave her head.

She held him by the balls for only a moment, then stroked his length. Playing for time. "All of a sudden I got to thinking of a story I heard about a woman who drowned in the shower giving her boyfriend a blowjob, and I realized I have so much to live for…"

Barry, his ass and back pressed against the stall, nudged with his hips and she nearly lost balance. "That's an urban legend and you know it. Anyway, the water isn't even touching me, it's all going down your back."

She looked up at his pained expression. He teetered on the edge and she – quite literally – held his fate in her hand. What the gossip sites must be willing to give for this visual.

"Tell you what," he then said when she didn't respond right away, "how about we try something more in tune with aquatic sport?"

"Like?"

He helped her stand and kissed her, exploring her backside with his hands while his hard-on grazed her thigh. He grabbed the condom set on the ledge by her bottle of body wash and positioned her so the spray hit them sideways. "Put your foot here." He indicated the narrow seat built into the shower fitting. She thought it odd at first, but noticed the position gave him better access.

*Ah, yes,* she thought when he entered her, *this I like.*

* * * *

They toweled each other off, just enough to keep Steffi's sheets from total soak. Given the late hour, it didn't take long for Barry to drift off to sleep, but the day's activity – in and out of clothes – left her wired and restless. She preferred not to use pills, but conceded to herbal supplements when necessary. Not bothering with a robe, she padded naked into her kitchen where she kept a bottle of melatonin.

A smile quirked up her lip at the sight of Barry's laptop, set crooked on her breakfast table. Often when he finished with it he was careful to shut it down and pack it into its bag. They'd been so eager to get on top of and tangled with each other that he'd put it on the first hard surface they'd come across.

It flattered her to think he craved her enough that his writing came second in his mind, even for a short time. She worried, though, about how the computer sat so far off the edge of the table. It wouldn't topple unaided, but she liked all expensive things safe from falling.

After she found her melatonin and downed a capsule with tap water, she pushed the laptop toward the center of the table. The screen lit up to reveal an open document. Interesting that Barry didn't have password protection, especially if he used this thing to manage his RydeAlong stuff.

*I can't peek. I don't have permission.* She chided herself for nursing the temptation to check out Barry's work. She'd left him near snoring in her bedroom, so she didn't anticipate a surprise appearance. She'd also witnessed his studiousness during his driving downtime – sometimes the sounds of typing had floated from the living room to wherever she'd sat in the house, steady and rapid.

Was any of it gold, though? Dialogue and action to attract

a producer's interest?

She knew plenty about solid scripts. Elliot Voller had written brilliantly for *ViP*, and Steffi had anticipated each new episode and the further development of her character. During her salad days, she'd read a number of screenplays that had gone on to win acclaim and awards...only not with her performing in them.

One peek — a few pages — then she'd close the clamshell. If what Barry had written showed promise, she'd throw subtle suggestions into their next conversation for improvement or encouragement.

If he was indeed writing semi-autobiographically, her interested boosted. She wanted to know more about him and where he came from. He, unlike her, lacked a Wikipedia entry for easy reference.

She scrolled the document, formatted in screenplay style, expecting to see dialogue about Cuban customs and food or descriptions of South Florida suburbs. Her gaze lit on the name *Rafaela* and an action that had said female character disarming a bad guy with white lasers shooting from her fingertips.

Well, celestial energy beams, as Barry described. This looked more like an episode of *Danse Macabre* set within her story arc, but she'd not seen any of this in her scripts. *How did Barry get this?*

She pressed the Home button and got her answer in Barry's full name at the top of the page along with the episode title. *Fallen Angel: Angel Versus the FBI.*

"This fucking better be fan fiction," she muttered, yet in her heart she saw she had a spec for a spin-off program. She couldn't decide if seeing this made her feel good about her job security. Gabby and Randi hadn't said word one to her about launching a show off *Danse Macabre* with her character taking the reins. Spinoffs were risky, though, and she considered the likelihood that ExStream wanted to see how well or how poorly the audience received her in the role. This *Fallen Angel* might happen regardless, with another actress cast.

That didn't explain why Barry was working on an episode of a show that had yet to exist.

She minimized the window and hovered the pointer over several folders. If she clicked the email icon, new messages might appear and clue Barry in to her snooping. *Damn it.* She wanted to know what was going on.

She spotted a yellow icon resembling a sticky note and double-clicked. A larger square popped up with a reminder to ask Randi Marsh about *Danse Macabre* and how heavily they were allowed to lean on that show with regards to references. Steffi imagined if she had accessed his email she'd find a lengthy back and forth between him and the old lady.

"You ass-kissing sack of crap." No wonder he insisted she show up to tomorrow night's party. He intended to hang-on and schmooze his way into a writing gig at Too True Productions. All that talk about his "art" and desire to bring a personal story to life onscreen…pure bull. Barry wanted the Hollywood high life like every goober stepping off the bus from Nowhereville, and what luck he had fallen into this temp job driving Miss Crazy.

He had told her he wasn't a star fucker. An opportunist, on the other hand…

She turned and reached for the junk drawer by the sink. She used it to store coupons that would soon expire, nail clippers, scissors, pens with little to no ink, and once in a while she'd find something useful.

Like a thumb drive.

She jammed it into a port and saved a copy of the script, then made sure to right all the windows to where they were when she had woken the machine. Leaving it to sit in its original position, she padded to her home office, opposite the bedroom where Barry slept unawares, and closed the door.

After firing up her laptop, she inserted the drive and began to read. One advantage to being an actress, she'd spent years honing excellent memory skills.

* * * *

The suit worked for the party. He'd balked at first when Steffi insisted he wear it—"It's paid for, might as well," had been her argument—but when he thought again of all the people expected to show, he realized clothes made the man. He was a starving writer, but what would showing up in frayed jeans and his favorite hoodie accomplish? He wanted a successful career in the industry, and had to appear at this shindig meaning business.

People like Randi Marsh...well, she'd paid her dues and then some, and therefore reserved the right to show up looking as she damn well pleased. When he escorted Steffi—lovely in a dark green, spaghetti-strapped bandage dress with matching flats—into the restaurant his gaze zeroed in on the former rock queen. Randi stood out in her cherry red vinyl jumpsuit and calf-high black boots, a fresh streak of pastel color in her hair. She waved a hand holding an egg roll at them, but Barry refused to make a show of being acquainted with her.

If he aroused Steffi's curiosity, he worried about blowing his big chance. They'd come here for her career, not his.

As he thought this, Steffi edged close and whispered in his ear, "You don't have to stick next to me the whole time, you know. If you want to mingle, network, go ahead. It's not often an aspiring anybody gets a break like this."

He pressed his palms against his crisp new slacks. The gift suit seemed tighter all of a sudden. "Any advice?"

"Don't act eager, and compliment your target like he's the father of the prom date you want to fuck," Steffi said. "It's all about stroking egos."

He needed to remember that line for later use and credit Steffi if it ever aired. "Thanks," he whispered back, but Steffi had already stepped from the entrance and filed into the throng, making a beeline for Randi. Damn. He'd hoped to chat up the director about his script ideas but settled for a trip to one of the buffet tables to survey the food and the crowd at the same time.

ExStream, Steffi had mentioned on the drive over, had rented the whole place for the night. It was all designer suits and cocktail dresses, slicks updos and twinkling jewelry as far as the eye could see. Not that different from the fated awards ceremony, just fewer tuxes and higher hems.

He recognized some faces — including actors connected to ExStream shows, but he knew them from other projects. Then there was Gabby Randall and Dash Gregory, who spotted him and moved closer to the buffet.

"Glad you came out." Gabby shook his hand and looked around. "I didn't see Steffi."

"She had Randi Marsh cornered a minute ago," Barry said, yet as he scanned the area he saw neither of them among the champagne sippers.

"Wonder if she's broken the news yet?" Dash murmured. Gabby flashed him a glance that threatened silence, but her features relaxed and she explained to Barry, "No sense keeping it under wraps, seeing as how it's been leaked. Eileen's about blabbed it to everybody she's met here tonight." The actress-producer jerked her head toward the end of the buffet line, where the assumed Eileen reared her head back in laughter at somebody's joke.

"ExStream put in a full episode order for a spinoff we created for *Danse Macabre*, and Randi's officially the showrunner," Gabby continued. "We sent over some rough footage of Steffi's story arc and they loved it. Lot of people think it's a better vehicle for her than her last show," she crossed her fingers, "so now Randi just has to convince Steffi to come on board."

Barry hoped he proved as good an actor as his companion, having known most of this already. Inside, he backflipped and fist-pumped and composed a list of people to thank when he received his first writing trophy. In the real world he nodded and beamed at what he felt were the appropriate times and offered his congratulations. "This is great news for your production company, too, having two hit shows on the site. It means you'll grow from here, right?" He wouldn't mind writing for a situational comedy, either, if Too True planned one.

Gabby and Dash exchanged looks and she cleared her throat. "In a manner of speaking," she began, and rubbed her belly. It was then Barry noticed she was one of the few nearby without a drink in her hand.

*Oh...*

"We found last month Gabby is pregnant, and we are over the moon." Dash's excitement showed in his voice. "It'll mean adjusting the calendar, but two shows are enough for the company right now. Gabby would be running both if it weren't for the baby."

"Not that I mind letting another person take the job," Gabby added. "Randi will be awesome."

"No doubt." That's one confirmation—the show was a go. Now to get Randi alone and secure a job. When the woman strutted by the table, examining the cheese and fruit selection, he made his move. Excusing himself from the happy couple, he slid to one side and reached for a toothpick to spear a few cheddar cubes. His arm crossed her line of vision, over a bunch of red grapes, and she lifted her head to acknowledge.

"You seen the guy with the bacon-wrapped scallops?" she asked, setting down her *hor d'oeuvre* plate on a clear spot. She'd taken a bit of everything available—adding one more nibble might cause the plastic to buckle from the weight. "Can't seem to corner him."

"I'll keep an eye out and grab extra for you."

"Thanks, hon. So, you hear the news? We're all legit now." She elbowed him and resumed munching. "Soon as I get back from touring I set up a schedule and we start shooting."

"Really?" That meant she must have at least a few episodes written and approved. "That's great. It's, uh, kind of what I wanted to talk to you about."

"Yeah. I gotta get you on some kind of mailing group for while I'm on the road, then we hold proper meetings like Gabby wants." Randi rolled her eyes as she spoke, leading Barry to guess he had to look forward to an unorthodox approach to show production. Still, the woman had to offer some structure otherwise the slipshod would show in the finished product.

"About that" —*oh, how to say it without sounding pushy*— "would I need to sign a contract...or something?"

Randi patted his shoulder and he caught a whiff of cocktail sauce and cinnamon. Randi clearly possessed an eclectic palette. "You bet. Everything's on the up and up with me. I like your writing, and as Gabby suggested I'll have a small team of house writers and some contracted freelancers who will pitch on a regular basis."

"I see." In those words, he heard his name excluded from the sure thing job, but a contract kept him close to the action. He'd just have to work hard to stay up front in Randi's mind.

"I ought to give Steffi a separate agreement for writing, too." Randi popped in a fried baby shrimp and chewed. "I was talking to her about the spinoff, and she's excited. She already had this cool idea about pitting Rafaela against a fed after a mass shopping mall shooting."

The air left Barry's lungs, and he nearly choked on the bite of cheese that ended up skidding roughly down his throat. "Excuse me," he said, and flagged down a server bearing champagne flutes.

"Details are still in draft, but the feds report a college kid lets loose after he flunks out. Rafaela thinks it's a false flag set up by the devil to distract the public from something bigger he has planned. That was all she had, but I'd keep my mouth shut, anyway. You know how it is, you don't want to tip your hand."

"I get it."

She lifted a beer bottle to her lips for a quick swig. "Sounds like a cool story arc for a series cliffhanger, either way. Maybe we'll get the two of you together to hash it out."

"Yes," he agreed. He'd love to see a story where Rafaela and the big bad man himself duke it out for millions of souls in a pivotal episode for the series.

Especially since he wrote it. Alone.

* * * *

*I see you, boy. Trying to springboard off me.*

She was still pissed, more so because he'd been so good in bed. It made getting even harder for her, and she told herself if *Fallen Angel* took off she'd have her share of groupies to fuck on cold nights. She read the ExStream fan boards, how people all over were willing to spread-eagle for Dash and his co-stars. Yes, men would put out for her. They did for most fan con mainstays, many twice her age.

She hung back, rocking on her feet in the periphery of two conversational circles. At her left, a few suits she didn't recognize discussed the Dow and the pros and cons of establishing an initial public offering—she assumed they came from ExStream's financial department. She didn't know much about money outside of what her accountant informed her, but as the company had been making noise for a while about getting a listing on the NYSE it seemed it was going to happen.

She nodded at them and smiled, then turned while sipping her champagne. Maybe, in light of her last binge, it made more sense to stick to soda, but she wanted to prove she could hold her liquor and act respectable in front of grownups.

Gabby stood to her right with Eileen Chester, who gushed in her ear about how much she loooooved the upcoming *Danse Macabre* arc. Funny to think how a few weeks ago this same woman had attempted to soften the blow of her show's cancelation with donuts and the promise of a sushi dinner. Which, by the way, she had never called back to plan.

Now, if she bent one way she feared Eileen might literally kiss her ass.

"You know I always had faith in you, right, Stef?" Eileen said. "*ViP* was a solid show, just a wrong place, wrong time kind of thing. Here…you and Too True pair up so much better and we can't wait to see what you do with *Fallen Angel*."

"Thanks." She kept her eyes trained on Barry and Randi the entire time. It helped stem the frustration of knowing ExStream saw nothing wrong with writing more checks to Gabby's company than sticking with her political drama.

"We all have to get together after the premiere," Eileen was saying. With *Danse Macabre*, Steffi knew, ExStream threw a big party and rented the historic New Beverly as the venue for showing the first episode. Nice to hear they had the change to spare for another star-studded production.

"Why not?" Steffi turned away from Barry and Randi for a second and smiled. "We'll get some sushi." Eileen took well to the idea, her long-ago promise to call forgotten. *Bleh.* "If you'll both excuse me," she added, without further explanation, and started toward the buffet. With each step, Barry's slow burn ratcheted up a degree. Up close, she'd be able to toast marshmallows by holding them near his flushed face.

"Speak of the devil," cracked Randi, who then picked up a crab wonton from her appetizer plate using her teeth and sucked it in with a quick inhale. "Catch y'all later," she added while chewing, and inched farther down the table.

"I'm ready to go, if you don't mind," Steffi said to Barry. "I've chatted with all the appropriate people, and ate enough stuffed mushrooms and feta dates to justify the gas money spent." She stuck her half-empty champagne flute in between two tureens of dip. "I've exhausted my social graces, and unlike Randi Marsh, I know when to quit."

The director stood far behind them now, dipping chips straight into the bowls and eating rather than using the spoons. The woman had no chill.

"Me, too." Barry gestured toward the exit and followed as she walked. "I'm not in the mood to party anymore."

"Headache?" Or guilt? *Forget about anger,* she decided. Yeah, she'd counted on Randi spilling about Steffi's 'story ideas' and had relished the reaction when it dawned on Barry that somebody else had pitched his script. He had no right to be upset, though, and the second he brought it up she intended to light into him. Never mind if they were speeding through the side streets of L.A. to get home or stuck on the congested freeway. No way in hell was he the wronged party here.

"I can't believe you broke into my laptop!" Barry slapped the steering wheel and rocked forward in his seat, like he wanted to headbutt the horn. Not a smart move in Hollywood traffic—she'd learned that the hard way and look how it ended for her. Stuck without a license...and with him.

"What's breaking in? You left it on my kitchen table without a password prompt." Who the hell waived that security measure on a computer? Five minutes in a coffee shop full of hackers and he'd be lucky to have enough in the bank to buy a *grande* mocha.

"And, knowing it didn't belong to you, you would have passed it without a second glance," Barry said. "It's simple courtesy. I don't go through your drawers or purse while I'm at your house."

"I don't plan to build a career driving people around L.A. and using you to make it happen."

That shut him up. Barry turned his focus to the road for the next few miles, his expression a mix of guilt and exhaustion. Still convinced he was wronged, but morose for having been caught.

"Steffi—"

"You were the guy who tried to steer me offstage at the awards. You kissed me on live television."

He nodded. "Let me explain that."

"Is it necessary?" she shot back. "I shouldn't assume this wasn't planned from the get-go? You didn't take advantage of my compromised position to weasel your way into Suzan's radar and land a job as my babysitter?"

"That's what you think?" he asked. "I used you…you believe everything I've done for you was self-serving."

She glared at him. He fixed on the road, turning away as the car rounded a corner. Well-timed, like he refused to meet her gaze lest his face betray his bluff. She saw the evidence of his opportunistic intentions—he had come into her life admitting his aspirations to write, and he dared to deny this.

"Well," she huffed, "I am paying you to drive me places. You make money. That serves you."

"That's a job. A salary. It's not what I'm talking about right now." He glanced at her, and just when she thought he prepared to turn down the road leading to home he executed a sharp turn in the other direction and swept into a parking lot before braking with a jolt.

A woman carrying a takeout bag skidded in her shoes near the front bumper, wide-eyed and cursing at them as she resumed a path to her car. "Learn to fucking drive, asshole!"

Barry ignored her, still fixed on Steffi. "Have you considered it's possible my writing talents got Randi's attention rather than my association with you? I met that woman before your lawyer offered me this job, which I took because I thought the exclusivity of one passenger worked better with my writing time. You don't know that I wouldn't have run into her again independent of this chauffeuring gig and landed a job on her show."

"We'll never know, will we?" she challenged. "All I see is a man who leveraged his position to forward his career."

"I see a woman who is upset for reasons I don't understand. I thought…" He let out a loud sigh, frowning as though the struggle for words weighed on his mind. "You're getting your license back soon and then you won't need me to shuttle you around town. You honestly expected me to go back to driving out-of-work actors and drunks from bars without the prospect of achieving my goals?"

"I never said I wanted to see you fail, or work a menial job forever. Do you have to follow your dreams by launching off my back?"

"I'm only doing that if you're collaborating with me on a screenplay...or I'm ripping you off. That didn't happen tonight, though, right?"

The eyebrow arched. Steffi wanted to return the look but her face felt numb.

"Barry, it's not like I intended to take it all the way to filming," she said. "I just wanted to scare the crap out of you, make you know what it's like for me."

Barry laughed without humor. He shook his head and resumed driving out the other end of the lot. "I'm still not seeing how you're the wronged party here. You made an ass of yourself on live television, and for most people, it's a career killer. You end up with a second chance any has-been would kill for."

"So now I'm a has-been."

"Now who's putting words in whose mouth?" he challenged.

*Ugh!* Who ever heard of an argument where neither participant made sense? Why weren't they home yet?

"What about everything else? You and me?" Barry asked. "You believe us sleeping together was a career move for me?"

Now, they came to the real question, the one weighing heavier on her mind since she discovered the contents of his laptop. "I don't know what that was, aside from enjoyable." Yeah, no sense lying about him being lousy in bed. She wasn't that phenomenal an actress that she was capable of faking her pleasure. It explained why she hadn't lasted very long in the soaps.

"Well, thanks for that, at least," Barry muttered. He turned the car into the Hills. Closer to home, and freedom.

It felt like their anger sucked the air out of the car and she had trouble breathing. She wanted to leap out into the thin California smog and fill her lungs, then shed her clothes and scrub away her frustrations in a long shower.

Barry…let him do whatever, in a different room. No more nookie. Going forward, he was the driver and nothing else.

Once in the garage and out of the car, Barry shot around the front and into the house through the always-unlocked side door. By the time Steffi untangled herself from the seat belt and emerged he reappeared in the doorway with his bags.

Probably heading out to write away his frustration. "What if I need you later on? To drive, of course."

"Call somebody else. I quit." He brushed past her to toss his things into the back seat, then glared up at her. "What?" he demanded. "You honestly think I want to hang around somebody who doesn't trust me?"

"Trust… It's not like you're putting my underwear on eBay. Come on." Angry as she was at him right now, this unnerved her a bit. Never before had anybody under her employ resigned on the spot. She'd fired her first agent after realizing his incompetence, and when she discovered the firm she'd hired to handle her social media had taken her money without doing the work she'd dumped them and resumed control of her accounts. People didn't leave her, and now in the space of a month it happened twice.

"No," she said.

He side-eyed her. "Excuse me?"

"I mean, our relationship is going to change, go back to what it was. I'm mad, but I wasn't planning to fire you." Like hell she wanted to break in another driver, give another person access to her privacy. Barry took advantage of his position but at least he kept things out of the public eye.

"I can't stay here if we're going to tiptoe around each other for the next few weeks." He shook his head and slammed the back car door. "I've done enough holiday dinners where a cousin brought a significant other who became an ex the night before, and they spread the awkward around because they weren't able to move up their flight home. Three hours dealing with that isn't bad if you have pumpkin pie to ease the pain, but this…" He blew out a breath and looked at her as if to add *the fuck am I saying?*

"You can find another RydeAlong chump to cart you to your chichi boutiques and coffee shops," he added, and tugged at the lapel of his jacket. "I'll have this cleaned and pressed and sent back to you, as well."

"That's your suit, Barry. I bought it for you." Men didn't return gifts to her, either.

"No. I may not be rich, but I can afford my own clothes."

She wanted to counter how he'd earned the suit by working for her, but the steel in his glare kept her mouth shut. Instead, she backed up until her heels hit the steps to the side house entrance and watched as Barry backed the car into the street and drove away.

Inside, she found the tie that had accompanied the suit on the kitchen table, still looped and knotted as though Barry had tossed away a noose.

* * * *

Loud music, heavy and vibrating along the hallway, filtered from the door across the way. Barry shared the floor with a sometime actor who posed for tips in a Thor costume on Hollywood Boulevard on days free of auditions. For all Barry knew, the guy was part-vampire because Thor seemed to never sleep. Forever blasting his tunes and pacing the hall and bumming pasta off him.

Uncanny hearing, too. Barry crept to his door, careful not to hit the squeak spots, and held his key ring tight to prevent jingling. Thor greeted him anyway once he got his door open.

*Groan.* He wasn't in the mood to hear a lengthy soliloquy about the hot chick and her busty friend that Thor balled all weekend at their Santa Monica digs. Barry nodded, smiled and leaned hard to make like he wanted in, just him.

"'Sup?" Thor's surfer boy slash Marvel hero good looks had once inspired jealousy in Barry. The charm must only have gone so far in the biz if the man still lived here.

"Really tired. I'm going straight to bed." *Go away.*

"I bet. I hear Steffi Corden's good at wearing her men out." Thor chuckled. Had he the strength or interest to further engage, Barry would have told him to fuck off, and he came close when Thor ducked back into his apartment.

"Somebody stopped by while you were out," he called from the other side. "Said his name was Wilbur Grant, or whatever."

"You mean Grant Wilberforce?" Talk about a blast from the past. He hadn't talked to Grant since the conference at La Jolla, where the other man had gotten a book deal on a handshake and he a rash from unwashed hotel sheets.

Thor emerged with a square, yellow note paper pinched between his forefingers. "He didn't have your phone number and took a chance you still lived here. I wasn't so sure until the landlord confirmed you hadn't moved."

"Thanks. I'm sure it's nothing major." Barry figured it was an invite to lunch to brag about his amazing career. Why Grant had bothered to go to the trouble hunt him down baffled him, though. The city was full of almost-happens ripe for boasting.

Thor grunted a goodnight and slammed his door. Barry kicked his way into his place and set his luggage near the couch. Sharp handwriting alerted him to call a number ASAP, but the line below those instructions had his full attention and curiosity.

*Sold film rights, kept writer approval. Need a gig?*

He froze, his mind filled with memories of watching the Cubs win the Series.

# Chapter Eleven

When her work on *Danse Macabre* ended, the promotion machine began soon afterward. Suzan worked with Too True's marketing team to line up appearances on late night shows and interviews with the major entertainment magazines. One of them set up a Snapchat "takeover" which featured Steffi galivanting around Beverly Hills, shopping for the perfect outfit to wear at the new series premiere party. She thought it silly, filming short-attention span videos of herself trying on high heels that pinched her feet, but Suzan assured her later the comments were positive for the most part.

*In time, people will forget you were such a bitch to Dash*, is what Steffi expected Suzan to tell her. If anything, she imagined these social PR outings made Gabby come out like a saint. A woman allowing her husband's ex a plum role on her show...hell if *that* didn't scream Mother Teresa.

Three months after filming her arc, she attended Too True's splashy viewing party. She posed for pictures with ten fans, winners of a contest sponsored by ExStream, and mingled with executives who, once cold to her following *ViP's* cancellation, now treated her like the second coming. "I saw the rough cut of one of your episodes. Gabby def needs to submit you for the Best Guest Actress award," Eileen had gushed before downing her champagne. "You'd win it easily."

Hard to say this early in the game, and the thought of attending another award show gave her hives. Steffi nodded and stuffed her face with bacon-wrapped figs to keep a smart-alecky comment from slipping free.

With every trip to and from the house, she went with a different RydeAlong driver. Even after the suspension on her license was lifted she continued to use the service because she stressed less when she didn't have to concentrate on the road. Also, she found she liked the proximity of other people on these excursions—she talked to the drivers and came out of her shell. She learned how others trying to break into the industry struggled and gave them advice on nailing an audition or securing a meeting. Paying it forward, being the voice of experience she wished she'd had when she started out.

Grad students paying off loans, empty nest moms earning pin money, retirees…RydeAlong offered variety. She never questioned why Suzan and Donald let her use the app on her own rather than vet another regular driver for her. The days following Barry's departure had taken an emotional toll on her—she missed him more than she realized. She supposed having a long-term driver might begin a new cycle, but dating or even fucking another man held no interest for her right now.

Steffi asked each new driver if they were acquainted with Barry, and every time got the same answer. They'd heard of and from him through the company's internal message boards, but he wasn't a friend. It wasn't until the pickup on her first day working for Randi Marsh that she struck gold. The prospect of going to Too True's offices for the table read of the first *Fallen Angel* ep left her so queasy she barely finished her coffee. Far as she knew, Barry still had ties with the show and this could be the first time seeing him since he stormed out of her house all those months ago.

A young woman arrived at her seldom-used front door, wearing a black crop top and leggings dotted with tiny pizza slices. She introduced herself as Vinnie and opened the passenger door of her Mini Cooper to Steffi. Steffi felt like she had to hold her breath before ducking down into it.

"Barry. Yeah, who doesn't know him? He's a damn legend." Vinnie snorted. "He was the top-rated driver for

L.A. for the longest time. Who can compete with that? It'd be like trying to outdo Kobe in layups."

Steffi shrugged her shoulders inward, feeling the compact effect of Vinnie's cigar box of a car. She wanted to cross her legs but feared taking out the dashboard. One word, though, pierced through her anxiety during the drive. "You said 'was'?"

"My friend Lisa works for Blue Tartan Productions. They're filming *The Bleakest Spring* with whatshisface." Vinnie snapped her fingers. "One of those toity British actors, they all look alike. Anyway, she does RydeAlong in her spare time, too, and she's seen Barry hanging out. He's in tight with the book's author."

"Really?"

"We all knew Barry wanted to write full-time, and since he's been off the boards I guess he got his break with that movie. Lucky bastard."

*Yeah, lucky.* Even if it came to pass Barry wasn't involved in *The Bleakest Spring* as a screenwriter, Blue Tartan wasn't a bad place to be. He had to have substantial work to keep him away from chauffeuring spoiled starlets.

*Good for him.* Steffi meant it. She wanted him to achieve his goals. More than that, she wanted to congratulate him face to face, and her mood lifted at the thought. Sitting in a speeding tin can seemed less terrifying now, especially since they neared Gabby's building.

Vinnie gave a sharp turn into a wide space, almost hugging a Benz. "Uh," her voice turned sheepish, "you don't mind if I walk you in? I *looove* Randi Raucous. I won't bug her if I see her, but I'd kill for just a glimpse."

"Hopefully it won't come to that." Steffi laughed and glanced to her right, wondering how she'd shimmy out of the car without denting the Mercedes. "Come on."

They met Gabby, back arched and supporting a bowling ball of a child under her loose tie-dyed caftan, and leather-clad Randi at the front desk. Together they resembled the cast of *Mad Max Goes to Woodstock*. After Gabby wished them luck and Randi posed for a selfie with the giddy rideshare driver, Steffi followed her new boss to the back conference room to start her first official day on the show.

Inside, she surveyed the bodies already seated and sipping coffee. She knew a few co-stars from previous shows and events, and focused greetings on those new to her. The absence of one particular face, though, nettled at her until Randi directed her to the chair with her nameplate.

"He ain't here," Randi whispered as they took adjacent chairs.

"Who? You mean Dash?" Steffi's heart jolted. Not a complete bluff. She'd heard the possibility of Dash making a cameo.

Randi snorted. "I meant your boy toy, Jeeves."

"Oh." Steffi looked at the pod-coffee brewer, longing for a cup. Ooh, Blue Mountain blend. "So he didn't work out then?" Feelings mixed within her. Angered as she'd been at the discovery of Barry's spec script, she had taken time to read it. He had created a great story, solid dialogue. She saw herself in character saying the lines and not feeling embarrassed about it.

"Oh, Barry's great. We've scheduled his episode before the finale, just a few tweaks to align the story with the overall arc. You'll get the updated scripts soon," Randi said.

Steffi glanced at the nameplates, noting writers not involved in the premiere. "Shouldn't he be here, anyway?"

"Eager, aren't you?"

She ignored the tease. "Hey, I may not have been in the biz as long as you have, but I know how some companies operate." Too True, she'd learned while dealing with Gabby, arranged for all writers to attend table reads in order to polish future scripts and bounce ideas for episodes not yet written. Barry, being absent, stood to lose ground among his peers.

Randi tapped her copy of the screenplay, prongs removed from the holes, on the table to straighten the pages. "Barry opted to come in halfway. He's working on a film for Blue

Tartan, so that's keeping him busy."

That confirmed Vinnie's bit of gossip. She wanted to check her phone and see if the author of *The Bleakest Spring* was the guy Barry had talked of. If not, he must have lucked out to get such a plum assignment this early in his career.

He lingered on her mind throughout much of the read, and while she joked along with the cast and other staff her mirth came out forced. When Randi called it a day Steffi paged for Vinnie to come get her and waited in the lobby, nodding and smiling her goodbyes while everybody filed from of the building.

Randi came up with her helmet tucked under her arm. "I got an extra one if you want a lift," she offered.

"Suzan'll kill me." No lie. Once upon a time her agent had lost a client—a promising young actor on a hit medical drama—after he'd crashed the Harley he'd bought with his first paycheck. Suzan had it written in her representation contracts that she had to clear any and all risky modes of transportation, including hang gliding and water skis.

"Aw, live a little. She doesn't have to know."

Steffi shook her head. She acted well enough to land award nominations and critic lauds, but for some reason, Suzan always called her bluff. She'd know if her star client hopped on the back of a motorcycle, never mind if Randi was the most cautious biker chick in the city. She doubted it, though.

A familiar sardine can crossed her line of vision through the glass doors and Steffi stood. "Maybe next time. My ride's here. See you tomorrow."

She offered to buy Vinnie's dinner at the In-N-Out drive-thru but the younger woman declined with a polite smile. "I'm on a cleanse this week." Vinnie held up a clear drink bottle for effect, showing off the dregs of some dark purple concoction clinging to the plastic cylinder. "Got a nice cold glass of homemade cashew milk with honey and cinnamon waiting at home."

That brought back memories of starving for roles. Ketchup

packet soup and hard-boiled egg whites for every meal. "Now that I think about it, I ought to eat better myself. Stop there anyway, though. I owe somebody a favor."

She ordered a cheeseburger and a Neapolitan milkshake, then gave Barry's address to Vinnie. At least, she had the streets memorized, and she'd recognize the building when she saw it. She considered texting in advance to make sure he was home, but after so much time of non-communication it would feel awkward... Well, yes, showing up unannounced with a milkshake also ranked high on that scale. She had to do something, though, to let him know she was sorry for being shitty to him — even in the early days when she had bossed him to fetch McMuffins and vague coffee orders.

More than that, she wanted to see his face again, admire his body. They may not make love again, but her memory of him had faded a bit with time and she wanted something to take home for cold nights.

"Wait here a sec?" she asked of Vinnie, who shrugged and appeared uninterested in the mysterious beneficiary of the fast food. Steffi hoped her memory proved sharp enough to recall Barry's door, but when she rapped on it the one opposite her opened instead.

Out popped a buff blond surfer whose eyes widened with recognition. "Damn, we always figured he'd come crawling back to you," the man said in a Cali drawl.

*Ignore it. Breathe...* "Is Barry coming back anytime soon?" The shake would melt, damn it. This dude looked more the cold-pressed, kale juice type.

"Barry moved out, and on up." Dude made an upward wave motion with his hand. "Got a sweet screenwriting gig and an advance, enough to rent a condo near the beach."

"I see." Well, that narrowed it down to...the whole damn coast. Steffi thanked him and slouched away, slurping as she went. The swirl of chocolate, vanilla and strawberry in the shake caused each flavor to become unidentifiable to her palate, and in the end, she winced from brain freeze as she rejoined Vinnie.

"Meeting didn't go well?" the girl asked, a hint of sympathy in her voice as they pulled from the curb.

"Didn't go, period. He took off. I'm not sure if I'll ever see him again." She explained Barry's good fortune without mentioning his name.

Vinnie nodded, her eyes on the road. "Don't rule it out. You know what they say in the business. People you meet on the way up, you pass them again on the way down."

"Yeah." Steffi pulled hard on the straw, hoping at least she and Barry might move in the same direction for a while.

* * * *

"Okay, one more," Barry said to the crowd of faces encapsulated in his tiny phone screen, "and then I have to get back to work."

"Fine," Ana groaned. "Mister Big Shot Screenwriter needs to rehearse his speech in front of the mirror." Along with her, other siblings, nephews and nieces tittered in the background.

"Trust me, I prefer this view to any reflection of my old mug." Standing on the balcony of his new home, he switched the phone camera's POV to show his family the wide expanse of Pacific Ocean and Venice Beach sand that served as his daily inspiration. He didn't live right along the shore, but with a swipe on the screen he was able to enlarge the view to exaggerate his proximity. Oohs and ahhs sounded from the speaker as he panned a shot to include some of the eclectic shops near the beach and fancy cars rolling down his street.

"So when can we come visit, huh?" piped up one of Ana's kids.

"Any time you want." Barry changed the POV back and smiled down at his family. Ever since announcing the deal with Blue Tartan to adapt *The Bleakest Spring* with Grant, friends and relatives had clogged his inbox with good wishes and requests for favors. Autographs from the cast and premiere tickets ranked high on the list, but he made no promises. Even if the production company conceded to give him passes, he wasn't flying anybody to California on his dime. This job brought him some coin and prestige – not to mention a new agent negotiating an option on one of his original works – but he still needed to watch his budget. The move from the old hole in the wall to this roomier pad, still a one-bedroom, was his only luxury, one he intended to maintain for a while.

If nothing else happened for him at Blue Tartan, he had *Fallen Angel* as a backup. Randi liked his writing, and he was excited about joining the show as full-fledged staff once he was no longer needed for the movie. Only the prospect of running into Steffi unnerved him, and it was destined to happen soon. He wasn't sure enough time had passed yet to soften the hard feelings there.

"Hey, I really gotta go now. Love you all, and kiss *mami* for me, okay?" He hung up after an extended goodbye and loped back into his living room, where he slumped on the couch. His face ached from smiling and holding back his exhaustion from the day's work. His sister might argue how being a writer required little energy, but he had the experience now to debate such a point.

Adapting another person's story for the screen, in particular, gave him a headache at times. He and Grant would share credit on the finished product, but in reality he did the majority of the writing while Grant critiqued every. Single. Page. Of course, the book author's vision of the saga hadn't matched that of the producer and director, and in recent weeks the actors cast in the leads wanted their say with regards to dialogue. They possessed enough clout to get away with it.

Some days the view of the ocean did more than inspire him, for the gentle roar of the waves helped him keep his cool. He glanced at his laptop, open to the latest draft with Grant's notes, and decided to eat before tackling it.

Midway through his fettucine Alfredo – brand name

sauce, whole wheat noodles this time — his phone pinged to show a name he hadn't seen in some time.

*Mr. Spahn, are you available for a driving assignment this evening?*

This from Donald Quinton. Barry laughed at the message and set down the phone. He finished his meal, rinsed the bowl and grabbed a beer for the long night of revisions when a twittering noise signaled him to acknowledge the message.

He thumbed out his answer.

*Sorry. I've paused my RydeAlong activity for the time being.*

*Never say never,* he thought. If he had to return to rideshare driving to cover a bill or two, so be it. Even Helen, pleased with his good fortune, had conceded to let other drivers cart her to readings. For now.

No driving for him tonight, though, and he wasn't interested in the cargo he assumed Donald wanted him to escort.

As an afterthought, he typed.

*I can recommend a few drivers if you're looking for discretion.*

Seconds later, Donald's speech bubble percolated and the response appeared.

*I am aware you are not driving for RA, but this is a unique situation.*

*This has nothing to do with Steffi Corden. My client will pay double the going rate.*

"Hmm…" He *had* spent the better part of the day cooped up either here or in the broom closet of an office loaned him at Blue Tartan. A drive might refresh him, and he hoped Donald's client was quiet as well as discreet.

He accepted the gig and sent the texted address to his

maps app. Good, not the Hollywood Hills, but a nice neighborhood, nonetheless. The directions led him to a gated home on a cul-de-sac and a rotund figure waiting by the mailbox.

"Holy hell," he muttered as a pregnant Gabby Randall-Gregory waddled close and groaned into the passenger seat. Wrapped in a dark raincoat, she wore pale blue slippers, and Barry spied the cuffs of what looked like flannel pajamas.

"Hi, there. You'll have to forgive me. I didn't realize you were so far along…and that I was picking you up tonight. I'd have gotten out to help—"

*Holy crap, is she in labor?*

"Oh, I'm fine. And no, I'm not due for a while yet. I see the fear in your eyes. Your seats will be dry for this trip." Gabby laughed and pulled a good length of seatbelt out before clicking the buckle. "We didn't go public about the baby until it was inevitable I had to say something. Dash is kind of superstitious, and he didn't want the media hounding us twenty-four-seven."

"If you don't mind my asking…"

She held up a finger. "He's in New York, taping Fallon. I forced him to go. Forbade me to drive, can you believe that?" She snorted.

*So here I am.* Barry smiled and checked for lurking paparazzi before shifting to drive. "Where to then?" He assumed nowhere formal.

"In-N-Out. Doesn't matter which one, whatever's close." That was his first guess. "Drive-thru is fine."

"Yes, ma'am," he said. "Uh, I'd have been happy to get your order and deliver it. You didn't have to come out." Gabby also could have called any number of services to do the same without getting Donald Quinton involved. Why the runaround, unless it had something to do with his working for Randi and therefore Gabby's company.

*Or,* he thought right as Gabby opened her mouth…

"I know you're a smart guy, Barry, and there's more to

you being here than fetching a preggo lady burgers. I want to talk about Steffi."

"There goes my appetite," he muttered.

"What's that?"

"Nothing," he said, and turned out of Gabby's neighborhood toward Hollywood and the nearest burger joint he knew by heart. "Is something wrong on the show? Everything I've read said things are fine."

"So far, so good." Gabby gave the passenger side window a superstitious rap with her knuckles. "Randi has everything under control, and she knows to come for help if she feels she's in over her head. But she's a pro, and I'm confident she'll turn out a great show. Steffi, too."

"This is all stuff to say over a phone."

"Please bear with an aching pregnant lady, all right?" Gabby chuffed. "I'm trying to have a heart-to-heart conversation while not thinking about a five-by-five animal-style burger and cheese fries." She patted her bulge. "And this little bugger is kicking like it's the gold medal game against Spain."

"He's not pressing on your bladder, I hope? I just vacuumed the car this week."

Gabby ignored that. "Steffi hasn't clued me in to the exact nature of your relationship—"

"One doesn't exist. Anymore."

"But when I look at her I see she's fighting something. She's lonely, and while she's polite to everybody she doesn't hang out after hours or socialize. It's like she wants to hurry home but also doesn't rush to get there. You know what I mean?"

Barry pondered her words, thinking back to his time with Steffi. She'd been a homebody during her license suspension period, and he'd assumed that had been normal. When Gabby mentioned the different RydeAlong driver a day, though, it perked his attention.

"If she wants to hire drivers, that's her business," he said. "She doesn't need me."

He stole a glance at first opportunity, careful to side-eye the road. Gabby offered a bitten lower lip smile and a limp shrug in answer, suggesting she had no theory on why Steffi continued to employ drivers. It wasn't his business, anyway, and Steffi may have had her reasons. Show-related, no doubt. She wanted her mind clear to remember lines, or had her nails painted in such a way that clutching a steering wheel threatened to chip them.

Lame excuse, that last one, but thinking about it made the slog through Hollywood traffic more bearable, and once he got to the drive-thru speaker he added a milkshake to Gabby's lumberjack-appetite sized order.

"I don't question her motives, but I get that she longs for more than solitude," Gabby said, and rooted around in her to-go bag for fries. "I've also noticed she was more outgoing and content when she filmed her *Danse Macabre* arc."

"Different environment, right? Maybe she got along better with your crew and—" He stopped short of mentioning Dash's name, thinking it too sensitive to bring up to Dash's pregnant, possibly hormonal wife.

"People are people, and everybody at *Fallen Angel* treats her like a princess. They want her to be happy, because she's the show." He heard wrapping paper rustling as she released the aroma of a cheeseburger dripping with ketchup. "She's the reason they're working. No," she said after chewing down a bite, "she used to have this look in her eyes. A woman knows it."

"I see."

"Whatever transpired between you two…was it so bad that you'll never speak to her again?" she asked. "I'm not saying marry her, but it's clear to me you parted on unfriendly terms. At the very least, if you're willing to find a more amicable closure it might lift her mood."

Barry was tempted to ask why Gabby cared, but understood how Steffi's well-being affected her livelihood. A happy Steffi meant a productive actress, one capable of taking *Fallen Angel* through several years of success. If Steffi was distracted or depressed, it spelled a premature death for yet another star vehicle.

In the months since he'd left Steffi's house, he had thought of her often. He abhorred social media for the bulk of his time writing the *Bleakest* script, but once or twice curiosity had gotten the better of him and he'd checked her Twitter. She'd offered nothing personal beyond teasers of her new show and mirror selfies in a dress she'd considered wearing to a gala or premiere. In the same breath, his thumb would brush the screen to call up his text window and type out a greeting to her, but he'd then erase it.

In checking mentions of and comments to her, he had seen few fans remarked on her social life. Any talk of her mystery kissing partner had ceased when the latest celebrity scandal had exploded, and the people at Blue Tartan abstained from getting personal with him.

Like he had the time to date.

They reached Gabby's home, and this time he helped her out while the car idled in park. "I can see myself to the front door, thanks. I need to walk, even though my ankles feel ready to burst." She clutched her food bag and slurped hard on her shake. "Give it some thought, anyway? Steffi hasn't gone all diva, but I don't know if this bleak mood will get worse."

"I will. I owe you all that. You and Randi gave me a break I didn't think I'd ever get." With a heartfelt goodbye, he pulled away from the cul-de-sac but paused the car on the side of the road, thinking a moment. It was a bit late in the evening, but not too late to put out a certain night owl if he happened to pop in for a brief visit.

After swiping his phone screen to wake it, he punched in a search.

# Chapter Twelve

*The hell was that?*

Steffi had been dozing in front of the television, her phone balanced on one thigh. She shifted whenever a notification caused the device to vibrate, but otherwise she seemed to teeter closer to unconsciousness with each passing minute. Visitors didn't come to the house unannounced — a neighbor would knock and Suzan had a key — so the sound of the doorbell threw her.

It *bonged* again, and she realized somebody was waiting for her on the front steps. She groaned. What was the point of owning a house in an affluent area designed to repel salesmen and strolling evangelists, especially at...*crap, the JWs must work a night shift now.*

"They better have food," she muttered as she padded to the door. Her stomach rumbled and she thought about the McMuffin she'd gotten earlier but neglected to eat. She decided to nuke it after she got rid of whoever, but when she opened the door to a large Winchell's box her appetite shifted.

She hated how her body betrayed the irritation she wanted to project. Seeing Barry with an 'aw shucks' smile and a box of sugary goodness set her blood flowing to all her perky spots. She longed to grab him by the collar and yank both inside for a late-night feast, when common sense dictated she should shut the door and remember how he had walked out of here, after leveraging his association with her to get a better job.

Nothing different than anybody in Hollywood would have done, she knew. He wasn't going to be her driver

162

forever, and she had to admit Barry calmed her, which in a way made it possible for her to slowly regain the respect of those in her industry.

Barry grasped the box with both hands and cleared his throat. Her reverie faded and she turned her attention to him. "Are you fundraising for church?" she asked.

"I haven't been to mass in years. Don't tell my mother." He sniffed, though, it was pleasant out. "I was on my way home and I passed a Winchell's, and remembered how many donuts I'd sneaked from your stash. I figured I should pay you back."

As far as lame excuses and peace offerings went, this ranked high in both categories. "You had kitchen privileges, you know."

"Everything but the buttermilk bar, you said, under pain of death. I took two while I was here." Barry gave her a meek smile.

"You son of a b—"

He held up the box. "There's three in here. The rest is all French."

"Get in."

She moved to one side, snatching the box away and marching it back to the TV. When Barry didn't follow, she waited and he appeared with a few paper towels.

"I haven't seen this show in forever." He nodded toward the set and perched on the recliner, close to her spot on the couch but not so much that they could touch. They were almost in the same position as when they had met. Well, not quite...but Steffi chose not to count their onscreen kiss since she hadn't been quite herself.

"I was too young for it the first time around." Her gazed fixed on the set and she let out a small laugh when a large man entered the bar scene and everybody called out his name. "I guess now I'll have to stream it, since it'll be coming on while I'm working."

Barry opened the box set on the corner table and took a cruller. "This one screenwriting class I took, we had an assignment to write an episode of a past or current sitcom. I chose this one."

Steffi arched an eyebrow. It sounded like a lazy assignment, akin to writing fan fiction, but she wasn't a teacher so what did she know?

"Instructions were simple. Write a twenty-two-minute script and stay as close to the spirit of the show. No crossovers or weird paranormal occurrences if the show wasn't sci-fi. So no special guest appearances by the Simpsons." He smirked. "I came up with a story where Diane came back to the bar after her Hollywood career tanked, and she and Sam kept missing each other at every turn. All the barflies tried to help, but it was the basic comedy of errors."

"Okay. So…she wanted her old job back, then?"

Barry lifted his hands, defeated. "Hell if I remember. I'm just yammering because I'm trying to keep things less awkward."

"Easier to do that if we just eat our donuts and be quiet."

"You think so?" He laughed, which lightened the atmosphere, though, he sounded a tad hollow. "Because I haven't been this uncomfortable since the night of junior prom when Lisa Scobee's dad cleaned his hunting rifle in front of me while we waited for her to finish crimping her hair."

"Yeah. You seem to have that deer in the crosshairs look," Steffi said with a smile, and licked up the sweetness lingering on her lips after her last buttermilk bar bite. "I don't own a gun, so the only thing I can polish off in front of you is the rest of this box." Nothing more. Not even an acting trophy to show off. Sad.

Rather than finish her sweet in two bites, she set it aside. "I was in the wrong, by the way, snooping on your laptop. I had no right to go through your files, especially not to copy one for my own use."

"It's okay—"

"It's not. It's theft," she insisted. "I'd get ticked if another actress worked on a tip to steal away a role I wanted." She tried to think of a more comparable scenario and failed. Video piracy? Sure, it affected her at some level, but she had trouble understanding the total impact on the industry.

Barry nodded and finished his donut. "What you read isn't close to the finished product, anyway. Randi had me rewrite the whole damn script, and in the end she brought on a writer to buddy-up with me. You probably know more about that storyline than I do at this point."

She laughed, then, "So I'll see you eventually, on set."

"I hope we'll get to talk more, not just pass each other in the halls like ex-bestie teenagers." With his elbows resting on his knees, Barry threaded his fingers together. Steffi saw flecks of dried sugar he hadn't yet licked away and felt the need to help him there. She remembered the way those hands had touched her, brought her pleasure. The added sweetness tempted her.

"That would be...nice." She cleared her throat and sat up straighter, willing him to look up at her. "When do you come back? Randi never said."

"In a few weeks. That's the plan."

"Okay." The air, or the lack thereof, stifled her. Sugar and whatever else Winchell's put in their pastry coursed through her veins and jacked up her heartbeat. Her knee bounced on its own, impatient, as though urging her to make a move.

"I was thinking," she continued, "maybe when you're ready we could...carpool to the studio."

Up went one eyebrow, along with one side of his lip.

"I don't drive much anymore. Too stressful." She shook her head. "But if you want to trade off, or I could cover your gas. I mean, if you're interested at all."

She looked down and realized Barry had taken her hand. Their connection warmed her, churned her insides filled with sugar.

"We can arrange something," he said and moved to sit next to her. He put his arm around her and squeezed her tight to his body. "If you like, I'll bring breakfast. Maybe a

McMuffin."

"What kind of a McMuffin? There's more than one."

His body shook with mild laughter. "You should know by now."

She chuffed along with him, sitting together as the next classic TV show came on the air. They watched through the night, as though it were the most natural thing to do.

* * * *

*Several months later*

No need to check a clock when the phone pealed for attention. It was dark o'thirty, way too early to function much less speak to another human being. Had she the energy or willingness to answer, the person on the receiving end stood to get an earful of curses.

Blessed silence followed after two rounds of the musical ringtone, but it was short-lived. When the phone rang again Steffi — face down in bed, eyes pinched shut and face buried in her pillow — slapped the bedside table for her evil communication device and growled into it. "What?"

No voice. Just music…coming from the other side of the bed.

Steffi elbowed Barry, her command unspoken yet understood once he startled awake.

He groaned and turned over, shifting to spoon her while the phone continued. "The fuck's calling this early?"

"Find the fuck out. Make it stop, and cut whoever it is out of the will." She rolled to her side, facing away from Barry while he answered. His words came in fits and groans, and Steffi listened half-heartedly as the one-sided conversation of "yeahs" and "uh-huhs" blended with the remnants of a dream.

After an extended moment of silence, she found being kept in the figurative dark more annoying than an unwanted wakeup call. She nudged Barry again. "So who was it?"

He shifted and spooned her, bringing his body heat to her

side of the bed. "Oh, just Ana. She watched the nominations this morning and wanted to congratulate you for getting one for Best Guest Actress."

"Aw, that's nice of her," she muttered and fell asleep again.

* * * *

The rest of the morning's sleep plunged her into near comatose levels. After rising on her own and fixing coffee, she met Barry out on the back patio, surprised to hear him mention how the phones had continued to jangle with congratulatory text messages.

"Suzan said she's stopping by with champagne and OJ, after she lines up a few radio station phone calls for you." He kept his gaze on his screen.

More than that, her agent wanted to show off the humongous diamond solitaire Donald had given her a few weeks ago. Steffi sipped her coffee and prepared her sanity for the onslaught of pictures she'd have to look at—poofy-sleeved dresses and sausage curl hairdos. Curse Suzan for having no sisters or cousins available to step into the maid of honor role.

Well, make that *matron*, assuming Barry's joking suggestion they elope to Vegas played out in reality. When Barry had proposed he'd offered to buy a nice ring with his next advance but she'd nixed the idea, saying she preferred to spend money on a new home. She snuggled next to him on the padded wicker loveseat while he scrolled a few possibilities, homes in the Hills that could accommodate a writing studio for him and a spare room for guests...or a nursery.

She kissed his cheek. "I'm guessing *Danse Macabre* is leading the nominations this season, too?"

"I think another show tied, but they're in the double digits, so I doubt ExStream has any complaints." He thumbed to another screen to show her the rundown. The show had nods in all the major acting categories, and multiples for writing and directing, and a host of technical nominations. The names rolled past in a bright blur until Barry paused at her category to give her a look at the competition.

*What do I care, anyway?* She sighed and returned her attention to the view. For once in her life, she felt secure in her career. *Fallen Angel* launched on ExStream in a month, and most of the critics previewing the first season had nothing but praise. Randi had Barry working on an arc for the next set of episodes and his mind bubbled over with ideas — on top of that he was deep in revisions on a movie optioned by ExStream, one of the first for their boutique studio. Steffi looked forward to traveling with Barry on the film festival circuit when her schedule allowed it.

Award or no award, she knew she had won plenty these last several months.

Barry's voice brought her slowly back to the present. "Do you think I should ask her?"

"Hmm?"

He shook his head and laughed. "That coffee had to have kicked in by now."

"Sorry. I'm somewhere else. You're talking about Ana?"

"She wants to come up for the award show. I told her I couldn't guarantee a ticket to the ceremony, but I remembered Mags still hires for seat fillers. You think Ana would want to do that?"

"I think Ana would explode into confetti if she were sat next to her favorite actor," Steffi said, thinking of her first conversation with her soon-to-be sister-in-law, all the squeals and celebrity worship that had left her ears ringing. It was cute, though, but the thought of Barry's large family coming to L.A. for a wedding frayed her nerves. Vegas was sounding so much better.

"Anyway," she added. "I don't know if I want to go this time. Last year was embarrassing enough."

"But fortuitous." Barry draped an arm over her shoulders and he pulled her close for a kiss. "You realize if you hadn't hijacked that limo we never would have met? If you'd gone back to your seat during the show they would have moved me somewhere else."

"A little bad behavior goes a long way," she agreed. "Well, if I'm not asked to give out an award what's the point? The guest categories are rarely televised."

"Less pressure for you."

She twined her fingers with his. "Even less if we watched from, say, the honeymoon suite at the Wynn?" With her free hand, she finger-walked a trail up his arm. "Order in some pizza and craft beer and sit in our underwear while Gabby gives another speech."

"You put it that way, it does take all the fun out of having to rent a tux."

"I love you, writer man."

"I love you, angel."

They kissed again to seal the deal and by the time Steffi finished her coffee, they had a room booked for awards night, the number of the chapel that married Gabby and Dash and a promise from the other woman to keep their secret. They toasted their future with the last swallow of coffee and sat together in a quiet moment, savoring a respite from the call of Hollywood lighting their respective phones.

"When I came to California I gave myself a five-year deadline. If I couldn't find work, I promised to go home to teach," Barry said. "Year five actually started a short while ago. So glad I made it with time to spare."

"Speaking of spare time." *Nudge, wink.* "Suzan's going to be a few more minutes…"

No need to elaborate. Laughing, Barry chased Steffi back into the bedroom to give her his congratulations.

# Finish What You Started

## *Excerpt*

## Chapter One

*April, 2006, Las Vegas*

Gabby Randall stood at the window of their fifteenth-floor suite at the Fitzgerald Hotel and Casino, looking out at the blinding lights of Fremont Street. Thousands of them, maybe a million, blinked in rapid succession, simulating waves and fireworks and starbursts in colors she hadn't realized existed. Down and to her right, a two-story tall neon cowboy winked and waved to passersby from his perch at the Pioneer Club. Bright yellow piping outlined his checkered shirt and knowing leer, and if Gabby moved one inch to one side or the other she could swear his eyes took on a sinister glow.

He stared at her, accusing her, as though to say *Shame on you, girlie. Eloping without telling nobody.* She wanted to turn away, but his eyes proved too hypnotic to resist.

"Shut up. I'm an adult," she muttered, and blinked to break the spell. The cowboy had a name. The clerk at registration had said as much, but it'd gone right out of her head, replaced by choruses of nearby jingling slot machines as Dash had given him two fake names and paid cash for the room.

She looked past the neon smirk and studied the vibrant patterns of one hotel's marquee. A thought occurred to her about the lights—how would anyone know to check for burnouts and replace the bulbs if the signs ran twenty-four-seven? Did the hotels each hire a specific person to stand on bulb duty? Were they like Christmas light strands, in that if one was faulty then the whole thing didn't light up?

Why she pondered this, of all things one wondered about Vegas, she didn't know. She took a deep breath and decided that her mind chose to focus on inane observations to calm her nerves.

It had less to do with coming to a strange city than it did with this being her first night alone with Dash. Her first night alone with any man, for that matter.

She'd never visited Las Vegas before, though she'd entertained a number of invitations from event planners. Her parents and managers, as devout in their Catholicism as their business savvy, had refused on her behalf time and again. No conventions or junkets unsanctioned by the network, or them, for her. Definitely, they didn't want her involved in a cheesy celebrity magic show or publicity stunt. Vegas might as well have been situated on the outer rim of Hell.

Now, their say mattered little. She'd turned twenty-one the previous week, on the same day her contract with Randall Talent had expired. Marie and Walter might remain family, but they no longer made decisions for her, business or otherwise. This included her most important one to date—her wedding to Dash Gregory.

*Gregory.* She was Gabby Gregory now. Or perhaps she

should hyphenate to Randall-Gregory, and use her given name, Gabrielle. Maybe that would make her appear mature, and more professional when she met with prospective agents to help her transition from TV ingénue to a place behind the camera.

In her left hand she held the current issue of *People* Magazine, the cover of which featured her with the other five principals of *Wondermancer High*, the television show that had served as her work and home for the past six years. In her right, a marriage certificate affirming her union with Dash Gregory bent in her tightening grip. It had happened only an hour ago, and if she brought the paper closer she could smell the printer ink. Her thumb brushed the black-marker signature of the minister, a middle-aged Johnny Cash impersonator with authentic sideburns and a paunch. Dash had insisted using a fake Elvis seemed too cliché, and that his late father—a Cash fan—would have gotten a kick out of it.

Gabby had conceded easily. She'd have stood before a showgirl in all her ostrich plumage and glitter if it meant a legitimate marriage. The Cash impersonator hadn't recognized either of them, which was good. He didn't fit their show's demographic, and apparently he didn't have a teenager who forced him to sit in front of the set every Thursday evening at eight.

She set the license on the nightstand to prevent further creases, then focused on the magazine. *Good Luck, Graduates!* read the headline, in reference to the series finale due to air next month. Sadness barely touched her as she recalled the emotion and angst which had pervaded the set when they'd filmed their final scenes. Relief was more like it. She'd played the part of Tula Truebend for six seasons, and as far as the country knew, her real life mirrored that of the prim, straight-A student aspiring to the upper echelons of the magical world. Hardly. Her grades, passable enough to let her continue acting, wouldn't get her into Harvard. She hadn't planned on college, anyway.

With the series behind her now, she couldn't wait to pursue a career as a screenwriter and producer — to create rather than regurgitate. First order of business — develop a project for Dash.

Of the six main actors on the paranormal-set show — created to capitalize on the success of the Harry Potter franchise — her new husband stood to suffer the most typecasting. While she'd played the brain, a pretty one to boot, he'd been the token geek. Glasses, perpetually bent wand, goofy laugh, and no fashion sense. The showrunners had neglected all requests to mature Freddie Grodin toward the end of the run, leaving 'Grody' to remain a beloved yet awkward and inept nerd in the eyes of *Wondermancer High* fans.

She promised herself Dash would have a long acting career, and not in variations of the same role. What the hell was taking so long with him, anyway? He'd gone for water...had he tried the Hoover Dam first?

The handle of their room's door jerked and rattled, startling her. On instinct, she clutched the full-length robe she wore tighter around her chest. When they'd stood exposed on Fremont Street, walking from the chapel to the hotel, she'd fretted over possible discovery from fans and paparazzi. Instead people had brushed past them, oblivious. Only in a city like this could that happen, she realized.

"Finally," Dash muttered and entered the room. "I hate these damn keycards. They only work half the time." A plastic bag, heavy with bottles and snacks, hung from his forearm, and he wore his favorite Dodgers cap pulled low over his face. Gabby smiled upon seeing it, especially since Dash really didn't need to wear it to conceal his identity. Without the taped-up glasses and slicked-back hair the world saw on Grody each week, Dash as himself resembled nothing of the character he played. She envied his ability to roam free.

No, Dash was gorgeous with his clear blue eyes and a hint of stubble shadowing his firm jaw. He removed the cap and ruffled his short hair, adding to his adorably scruffy look.

"I'm glad you're back," she told him, and approached him for a hug. "I don't like being here by myself."

"Hey." He took the magazine from her and set it next to the license, then enveloped her in his arms. He felt safe, warm. "It's okay. Didn't I tell you we'd be all right? It's official, we're married, and there's nothing anybody can do about it."

"I keep thinking somebody saw us downstairs." Visions bloomed in her mind of photographers stalking each floor of the hotel, disguising themselves as room service. Fans pulling out their cell phones or running for the nearest pay phone to tell their friends, or worse, announce it to the world via their MySpace pages and that new site, Twitter. Guess what…we saw Tula and Grody in Vegas! Why would they be here, checking into the same hotel room? *Ooooh!*

Friends tell other friends. Somebody knows a guy at the Enquirer. He calls his contact in Vegas. Somebody calls her parents…in three seconds the SWAT team will kick down their door…

"Gabby, you're shaking."

"I just want to be a married person for one night without the world knowing about it."

Dash chuckled. It vibrated throughout her body, making her very aware of him. The robe slipped open and her breasts, hidden by a sheer layer of satin and lace, pressed against his body when he drew her against him. Her nipples hardened, anticipating his touch.

They hadn't seen this much of each other during the year they'd secretly dated. They'd kissed, a lot, and enjoyed a quick grope over clothes in between scenes. She'd saved it all for tonight.

"We're fine, Gabby," he assured her. "We could walk the whole Strip tonight and nobody is going to notice us. There's enough in Vegas to distract people. In fact," he pulled away and she whimpered, "I thought we might stay an extra night."

"But we're going to New York tomorrow." An outsider might have viewed their wedding as spontaneous, but they'd put a fair amount of planning into this week. Marry in Vegas, then off to Manhattan to shop for an apartment. Stage and TV auditions for Dash while she met with agents to discuss her ideas for projects.

"I know, but you deserve a proper honeymoon, however short. It's not like we're broke and have to go back to work immediately."

"I know." Assuming *Wondermancer High* enjoyed a long life in syndication, they wouldn't have to work again with their combined income if they budgeted well. She wanted to work, though, and intended to distance herself from Tula Truebend.

He sat on the edge of the bed and kicked off his shoes. The white Polo he'd worn for the ceremony came next, discarded onto the carpet. Dash stretched his arms to the ceiling and Gabby marveled at the definition in his muscles. She couldn't wait to trace every ridge and curve.

"I was thinking we'd go see Celine or Elton, or Cirque du Soleil," he continued, shucking his pants and socks. Clad in his boxers, he scooted back to lie on the bed. "I'll get tickets for whatever you want. I got the room for two nights either way, and New York isn't going anywhere."

He patted the vacant side of the mattress and eyed her standing form. The robe's belt had come loose, exposing her legs and the red baby-doll barely covering her thighs.

"I'm not going anywhere, either," he added.

"Good." The robe slid to the floor, and Gabby crawled up the bed and moved flush against her new groom. Dash slanted his mouth over hers, and she melted into his embrace, sinking deeper into bed as he rolled closer. She explored the smooth planes of his back on down to his cotton shorts, where she longed to discover his better assets. Limbs twined, fingers plucked at straps and elastic bands, all the while she let her husband plunder her mouth with his tongue. She tasted the coffee they'd shared earlier and a hint of mint gum, clearly used to mask the strong drink.

She'd never felt happier, being with Dash. She was ready to put Tula Truebend behind her and act her age. She'd reveled in the simple act of buying this skimpy lingerie for her wedding night, enjoying shopping like a "grown up."

Her parents had kept her under constant watch during the show's run, having everything done for her. They'd paid her bills, chosen her outfits, and watched her diet. No more. She wouldn't think about them tonight.

The straps of her baby-doll drooped down her shoulders, freeing her body. Dash broke from her lips and kissed a trail to one breast, circling the nipple with his tongue. She shivered at the sensation, as though he set her every nerve ablaze with his touch.

He looked up with glazed eyes and a swollen smile. "Did you...?"

She nodded, and her silent affirmation that she'd taken her pill sufficed. She'd gotten the prescription in secret last month, in anticipation of their marriage.

Dash returned to her breasts for a full-on assault, nipping one while kneading the other. He shifted over her, allowing her to feel the fullness of his arousal. Gabby relaxed and let him take over. His every thrust against her sex, while still in his boxers, sparked her desire, readying her to become his in every sense of the word.

*No*, she thought, *we'll belong to each other*. When the shorts and her lacy thong came off and he entered her with one slow, guided stroke, she bit her lip to avoid crying out and focused on Dash above her, burying his face into the crook of her neck, cooing his reassurance that he would take care of her.

"You okay?" he whispered, his warm breath roaring in her ear.

"Fantastic. Are you?"

"Yeah." He laughed, giddy like, and pushed into her again. The pain subsided the longer they lay joined, but when he reached down for her clit she cried out. She was no stranger to self-pleasure, but having Dash touch her in this way brought her to climax much quicker than she had ever accomplished alone.

"Wow." He laughed.

"Sorry about that." She'd wanted to last, but his kiss soothed her guilt.

"I love you, babe," he said, and after a second his body shuddered. He bore down on top of her, and Gabby looked down his back to see his cute ass bob faster as he filled her. The increased motion dizzied her senses, and the heat enveloping her took her breath away. She wanted to return the sentiment, tell him she loved him as much, but the words caught in her throat.

Instead, she focused on them and tried something she'd read about in a how-to manual. With him deep inside her she tightened around him and thrust. *Oh, that's nice.*

Dash reared upward, his face pinched with pleasured pain, and cried out as he released. The warmth blossomed inside her, and they kissed away their afterglow, their hands sliding across dampened skin and fisting the sheets.

*I love you.* The words looped in her mind, and she hoped their connection strengthened enough for him to hear it.

Dash pulled away and they touched foreheads. His lashes brushed hers and he shook with quiet laughter. "I can't wait until bedtime every night, if it's like this."

She almost made a *Wondermancer High* joke—*It's nothing like the dorms at Huntington Hall.* Instead she nodded and kissed his nose. No references to the past, she decided. They weren't Tula and Grody, who only spoke to each other when Tula needed him to get her boyfriend out of a scrape.

She was Mrs. Gregory. Now and forever.

She took the comforting realization to sleep, Dash spooning her as they turned on their sides toward the window looking out onto Fremont Street.

"What do you think?" he whispered in her ear. "Stay an extra day."

"Sure." She'd prefer to spend all their time here.

She snuggled against her husband and watched what lights were visible until she drifted away, thankful the neon cowboy couldn't see them.

* * * *

He first heard the knocking sometime around six, as the clock by him read, and bolted upright in bed when he didn't recognize anything in the room. After a few seconds his memory kicked back into gear, and he checked on Gabby. She had shifted little in sleep, remaining on her side and snoring quietly.

*Still married, good. Wife here. Tired. Sleep more.*

Dash waited, then settled back into bed with his arm around her, convinced one of their neighbors was being summoned from slumber. He'd arranged for room service to wheel up breakfast at eight, and he saw no reason to —

A second series of knocks, more forceful, jarred him. He cursed. Either the front desk had screwed up the delivery time or somebody had the wrong room. *Damn it.* He'd hoped for at least another hour of sleep, then waking leisurely and making love to Gabby to work up their appetite before taking on the day.

Instead he slid out of bed, found his boxers, and hopped into them as he headed for the door. "Go away," he called out. "You're two hours early."

"Open this goddamn door."

*Fuck.* He knew Walter Randall's hot-gravel voice anywhere. How in the hell had he tracked them here? He and Gabby had told nobody about their elopement — no co-stars, no close relatives. Definitely no meddling parents. He'd trusted only Gabby with their plans.

That meant somebody along the way had pieced it together and ratted them out. No time, though, to consider the clerk at the car rental against the woman processing their license and ceremony fee at the chapel.

"Gabby!" called out a shrill female voice. Great. Marie

had come, too. Of course she had, she'd probably driven. Everybody knew the woman yanked Walter around on a leash. "We know you're in there! Open this door!"

"Huh?" The noise roused Gabby and she sat up, the sheets folded on her lap. She looked so adorable sitting there, bare-breasted with her hair sticking out in all directions. Too bad her parents had to show up and ruin what otherwise could have turned into passionate morning sex.

"Here," he whispered and tossed her robe on the bed. "Did you tell your parents we were here?"

That woke her up. "No!" She dressed hurriedly. "You never told me which hotel we were staying at, so how could I say anything even if I wanted to?"

The pounding and shouting increased into frenzied panic, and boiled Dash's blood. They were adults, for crying out loud. Never mind that they were his in-laws now, Marie and Walter Randall had no business horning in on them like this. They'd intended to break the news to family before alerting the media, yes, but they deserved at least one day to themselves.

He took a deep breath and unlatched the security chain, then opened the door. The two middle-aged talent managers—rail-thin and balding Walter in his trademark cords and elbow-patched jacket, full-figured Marie in one of her tropical explosion caftans—bustled into the space as though prepared to take down a drug cartel. Neither brandished a gun, but the umbrella Walter wielded like a ninja might have taken out an eye if Dash hadn't backed away.

"What the hell is going on here?" Marie demanded. She paced the room with a critical eye, no doubt searching for hidden cameras. Dash knew how Gabby's parents hovered over her, shielding her from the media and men and saturated fats. It was no wonder she'd felt somewhat inhibited last night when they'd made love. She'd wanted to get married, but Dash wouldn't have been surprised to find his wife holding back at certain moments.

Turning twenty-one, and freeing herself of her parents' grasp, was supposed to change everything. Yeah, she'd legally become an adult at eighteen like anybody else, but damn, her parents and that iron-clad contract…

Marie laid eyes on her daughter and gasped in exaggerated horror. "Holy Mother…Gabby, did you have sex with him? In a cheap hotel?"

"This is not a cheap hotel," Dash protested. Not for what he paid.

Gabby belted her robe and stood up to her mother. "That's not your concern. I'm an adult and I'm not your client anymore. Even if I were still your client, my personal business is not your concern. What are you doing here?" She folded her arms.

"You're still our daughter," Walter said, also scanning the room. For what — contraband, porn, other people — Dash wasn't sure. "And we care."

"She's twenty-one years old —" Dash began, but Marie silenced him with a barking reprimand. Then she cried out again, something crumpled in her hammy fist.

"What is this? Viva Las Vegas Wedding Chapel?" Her eyes bulged as she read. "Walter, they got married!"

Walter turned toward Dash, fury reddening his normally pasty complexion.

Dash smiled. "Hi, Dad."

"Don't you 'Hi, Dad', him. You put her up to this. You tricked her," Marie accused. She stormed around the bed, wagging her finger in anger. "Gabby has a whole career ahead of her, and I'll be damned if she ruins everything by marrying too young."

Too young? They were legally adults, for crying out loud! "You mean the way you did?" Yeah, he aimed below the belt, but Dash knew Marie's history, how she'd given up a promising acting career after getting pregnant with Gabby. How she and Walter had decided instead to give their children the opportunities denied them, all for the greater good of the family.

Dash knew this, because the Randalls reminded the cast of *Wondermancer High* constantly. Every time Gabby had shown signs of burnout or interest in something outside of acting, they'd played the sacrifice card and guilted her back to the set. He'd admit to himself or anyone else that he fell for her partly because he wanted to protect her from her parents. However, Gabby seemed to be doing well enough on her own at the moment.

"Yes, it's my career and my life," his wife said, "and only I have a say in how I manage both. Well" — she cast a loving glance at him — "Dash and I are a team now."

Marie's eyes narrowed to slits, stabbing invisible daggers at Dash. "You're lucky we didn't call the cops on you."

"For what? We eloped. We're married. I didn't have to coerce Gabby, because she wants this as much as I do."

"That's right, Mother," Gabby added. "You can't tell me what to do. Either of you. You're not my managers anymore. In fact, I'm actively looking for new representation."

Walter snatched the marriage license, waving the fisted paper in his daughter's face. "This is not a marriage. You marry in a church, with a priest, sanctioned by God. This" — the paper tore in his fingers — "is a farce."

"Hey, don't do that." Dash reached for the license but Marie, somehow getting the umbrella without him seeing, waved the pointy end at his face.

"I should have kept a better eye on you on the set. All this time I thought Reed would make a play for her, but no…it's always the one you least expect."

His and Gabby's co-star Reed was gay and in a relationship with a screenwriter, but he let it go unsaid. He wanted to laugh at this confrontation — it had turned from frightening to ridiculous. Perhaps Marie could salvage her acting career after all, and try out for batshit crazy mother-in-law roles.

"It's a good thing we hired that private detective when we did, though we got here too late to stop the wedding," Walter muttered.

"What!" Gabby stormed to Dash's side, looking as furious

as he felt. "You had us followed? What is wrong with you two?"

Her mother carried on, not listening. "It's no big deal, Walter. We can spin this. We'll call Wayne, and he'll get her an annulment…"

"You will *not*. She's my wife. I'm her husband. Which of these statements are you having trouble understanding?" He talked slowly now, his voice rising. Gabby had warned him that her parents wouldn't take the news well, but he didn't expect to see complete denial and scheming to undo everything while he stood there in front of them.

"Gabby, where's your bag?" Marie paced the room. "You know what, forget luggage. Get dressed. We're leaving."

Enough of this shit. Dash palmed Walter's shoulder and steered him toward the exit. "No, you know what? *You're* leaving. Gabby and I are on our honeymoon and don't want to be disturbed. We will call when you're ready to talk like civilized people."

"Dash, wait."

The plea in her voice chilled his blood. He recognized the tone—one of acquiescence. He'd heard it on the set often, every time Gabby'd resisted a scene in the script or a promotional obligation. Her parents would talk to her privately, and seconds later Gabby would step back in line like an obedient—and chastened—little girl.

Walter shrugged free and glared him down. He stood a foot taller than Dash, but lacked upper body strength. If Dash had to get physical to defend himself, he would.

Gabby held out her hands, playing the peacemaker. "Let me talk with them, please?" She moved closer to talk lower. "Give me a few minutes with my parents, and I'll make sure they understand they can't push us around."

Dash glanced at Walter and Marie, and walked her toward the window, out of their earshot. Vegas never shut off—the lights continued their round-the-clock sequence of blinding patterns and waves. They ought to be here alone, looking out at the spectacle, kissing and planning which casino they wanted to invade.

"I don't want you alone with them," he whispered back. "They aren't speaking rationally. They think they still control you."

Gabby looked affronted by this. "You don't trust me to handle my parents?"

"Gabby, I love you. I know what they're capable of..."

Her face turned sour, and he changed his tack, "But you're strong. I just want to be with you."

The doubt remained in his mind. He believed in his wife, but he knew Walter and Marie. Since day one of her career, they'd hovered over Gabby and counted every penny. They had other clients, but none as successful as their daughter. Her independence threatened their livelihood.

She grasped his hand and he saw her dark eyes glass over. "We will stay together, Dash. I'll talk to them, we'll straighten this out, and after they're gone we can go on with our lives. Please."

Dash sighed. He wanted to start married life off on the right foot, and keeping Gabby happy remained top priority. He kissed her cheek and stormed past Marie and Walter to where his clothes lay on the floor. He grabbed his jeans and shirt and quickly dressed, making sure he had his wallet, flip phone, and the room keycard. "I'll wait outside," he then said.

"You'll wait downstairs," Walter countered.

"No fucking way." Before Dash could protest further the older man had him by the arm.

"What?" He pushed when Dash resisted. "You don't trust us with your wife?"

A trick question. Either way he answered, Gabby might take something from it that he didn't necessarily intend. "Fine. I'll be in the lobby," he said, looking right at Gabby. "I love you. Call my cell when you're done."

Gabby nodded, biting her lip and wiping back tears. With one last look at an agitated Marie and Walter, he closed the room door behind him but lingered only a few feet away before walking slowly toward the elevator. Quite slowly.

After a few seconds Walter's face appeared as the door cracked open. "You can't fool us. We can see you through the peephole, Einstein."

"What difference does it make where I wait? I can't hear anything out here, and besides, you two aren't staying long." He folded his arms.

"Hey, we're in no hurry to go home. You want to hang out here, okay. We've got all day in this room with our daughter." Walter sneered, his canines prominent and ready to bite. Whatever, dude. If the Randalls wanted a standoff, he'd play, never mind how his bladder ached for release.

During the quiet pause of their stare down, Dash swore he heard Gabby sob in the background and made to rush forward, but her earlier plea sounded in his head. No. As much as he yearned to act the white knight, he trusted his wife. Gabby wanted to bring closure to this stage of her life and he wanted to stand by her.

That meant giving her space.

Walter's face remained lodged between the door and jamb, and Dash noticed they'd engaged the swing bar lock so he couldn't use his keycard and barge back inside if he wanted. Typical. To Dash, his father-in-law resembled the crazed Jack Torrence from the 'Here's Johnny!' scene in *The Shining*. He'd never unsee this.

"All right. I'm going, but I'll be back." Dash stormed to the end of the hall, checking back every few seconds. Walter surveyed his retreat all the way, saying nothing and not moving a muscle until Dash got into the elevator.

When the doors slid shut he let out a ragged sigh and reached for the button panel to get back out, but the car had started moving.

"This is a mistake." He hated that he had caved. Gabby might not see it that way, but his in-laws had no right to interrupt their honeymoon. Hearing Gabby cry made him uncomfortable. He hadn't known the Randalls to physically abuse any of their children or clients, but if they were desperate who knew what they might try, given the chance.

After an agonizingly slow descent to the ground floor, the elevator stopped moving and the doors opened to the lobby, not to the cacophony of slot machines and tourists wandering to and fro, but the collective flash of a dozen or more cameras. A head turned and a finger pointed in his direction. "There he is!" Then the scene turned into bodies, many running at him. "Dash, Dash, Dash…" Voices shouted from all directions, hands jammed microphones at his face. "Where's Gabby, and why did you take her from L.A.?"

"Did you get married, did any of your co-stars know?"

"How did you manage to keep this under wraps?"

The ambush disoriented him for a few seconds, and with the paparazzi so close, a few cameramen gathered behind him to prevent his escape back into the elevator. It worked — the doors closed before he could take a step back.

Normally, he tolerated the media, even the aggressive paps who recognized him out of his Grody guise and trailed him on his morning jogs, because what secrets can one expect to unearth while a TV actor runs through his neighborhood?

This time, though, he connected their presence with the arrival of Gabby's parents. Yeah, some photographers slept in trees to get the right shot, but he didn't doubt the Randalls had orchestrated this distraction.

He had to get back to the room, *now*.

"No comment," he said to the crowd over, and over, and squeezed through the throng, turning around to call for another elevator. The reporters refused to accept his dismissal, however, and pelted him with more questions.

He tuned them out, elbowing away microphones and lenses, pressing the up button until he chipped a fingernail. Over and over again. *Gabby*, he pleaded silently, *please be there. Don't leave me.*

"Dash, is there any truth to the rumor you've signed on to

a *Wondermancer High* spinoff?" asked a slender woman in a gray pantsuit.

What was she talking about? He was done with the show and everything related to it, save for Gabby. He brushed away the mini tape recorder she held close to his face. "No comment."

The doors of the second elevator opened and the crowd surged. Several people already occupied the car, but Dash pushed forward and shouted for his floor. The man nearest the buttons, his eyes bulging at the crowd, swiped at several numbers until the doors shut.

"Thank you," he breathed out, and sagged in one corner. He was sharing the ride with a group of senior citizens, all of whom stared at him with varying degrees of curiosity and fear.

Damn it, the reporter got in, too.

"What the hell was all that out there? You in some kind of boy band?" asked a man wearing a trucker's cap emblazoned with a chewing tobacco logo.

"What about Gabby, Dash?" asked the reporter. "Do you plan to work with her in the future? Are you two in a romantic relationship? How long have you been involved with her?"

"Shut up." Dash turned away from the group, wishing he actually possessed some of the powers wielded by the fictional *Wondermancer High* students. Given the choice, he could turn himself invisible, or change this annoying young woman into a coat rack.

"Are you aware her parents have been trying to renew their management contract with her? How do they feel about you being romantically involved with their daughter?"

*Well, duh. You should know the answer to that. Surely they tipped you off to us being here.*

"Excuse me," piped up one of the older women. "He never said he was the girl's boyfriend. It's not right for you to assume otherwise."

Dash's gaze panned the cluster of tourists. Everybody

looked at him, expecting confirmation. "No comment," he muttered.

"Did you marry Gabby Randall? Do you plan to marry her today? Do you—"

"Lady," broke in the geezer in the cap, "I think he wants you to cool it with the questions."

"Yes," agreed a second woman. A green visor sat on her silver helmet of hair. "Leave the boy alone. He's obviously exhausted by this third degree."

"Hey," the reporter snapped. "I'm doing my job here, grandma."

The golden girl didn't take kindly to the remark. "What you're doing is hounding the poor man, and you should stop. You're just like those vultures who drove Princess Diana to her death. Chasing her down that tunnel taking pictures. You so-called journalists have no class anymore."

"Oh, whose fault is that, really?" Voices rose with the car's temperature. "If people like you weren't buying up the tabloids for the news I deliver—"

"The Internet's gonna put you all out of work, just you wait."

Then the dam burst. Dash rubbed his temples as shouts of "How dare you!" and "I have every right..." volleyed between the reporter and her new detractors. By the time they arrived at his floor the old folks had her cornered, allowing him to escape.

From the distance he saw that their door was ajar, and he lost his breath. After a second he called out for Gabby and lunged headlong into the room.

Empty.

He checked the bathroom—no sign of her.

Nothing in the room remained of Gabby, except a scribbling on the hotel notepad left on the bed.

*I'm sorry. Please forgive me.*

He held it for the longest time, staring down at the bed

where hours earlier they had consummated their marriage, now wondering if they had another chance.

Behind him, the reporter thumped into the room, catching her breath. "Dash, where's Gabby? Dash?"

# More books from Totally Bound Publishing

Book one in The Devil's Prophets series

*To reunite with her kidnapped son, a reclusive bookkeeper infiltrates an outlaw biker club, only to fall for one of the members.*

little
white
lie

One little white lie
turned her universe
upside down

MADISON
NIGHT

*Sydney was being coerced into marrying a man she didn't love. Then Caleb crashed into her life and one little white lie turned her universe upside down.*

*Two recovering sex addicts. Two broken souls. One shared passion.*

Book three in the Beautiful Sinners series

*This party girl knows what she wants…but he is everything she needs.*

# About the Author

**Kathryn Lively**

Kathryn Lively is an award-winning writer and editor, avid Whovian, and Rush (the band) fan. She loves chocolate and British crisps and is still searching for a good US dealer of Japanese Kit Kat bars.

Kathryn is a regular contributor to the Sexy To Go authors group and enjoys the outdoors, when she's able to get out.

Kathryn Lively loves to hear from readers. You can find contact information, website details and an author profile page at https://www.totallybound.com/

Home of Erotic Romance